CATHERINE FEARNS is an author and musician from Liverpool, UK. Known for her award-winning *Reprobation* series of crime fiction novels, Catherine's music journalism and short fiction has also been widely published.

As a musician, she is a composer with Universal Edition and her solo albums are available from Blue Spiral Records. She also plays guitar and keyboards in all-female heavy metal group Chaos Rising.

Follow Catherine on Twitter @Metalmamawrites

Instagram @catherine_fearns

Website catherine-fearns.com

GW00499573

BOOK FOUR IN
THE REPROBATION SERIES

LAMB

of GOD

CATHERINE
FEARNS

Northodox Press Ltd
Maiden Greve, Malton,
North Yorkshire, YO17 7BE

This edition 2023

1
First published in Great Britain by
Northodox Press 2023

ISBN: 9781915179944

This book is set in Caslon Pro Std

For my parents

'It's not true, but I believe in it.
Well, I don't believe in it, but it's true.'

Umberto Eco, Foucault's Pendulum

'And Aaron shall cast lots over the two goats, one lot for the
LORD and the other lot for Azazel.'

Leviticus 16:8

Prologue

At the edge of things, a boy flies a kite.

'Elizabeth, look!'

He runs with it, clumsily, stumbling a little on the sand as he looks behind him, and then he throws, inexpertly yet the wind is so strong that the kite takes flight. Gaudy-coloured and shaped like an owl with outstretched wings, the kite darts and swoops, its flapping streamers unable to detract from its grace, before settling into position so that its eyes stare back at the boy.

He plants his feet and grips the handle with both hands, pulling it down taut against the wind, enjoying the feeling of control and balance as he battles against the elements. He looks around and the baby shares his glee. Wrapped up in her pram she looks up in awe, mouth wide open in delight.

'Pretty cool, hey Elizabeth?' he shouts. He knows she can't hear him, but still. Someone to share his exhilaration makes it all the better.

The boy, the pram and the kite cut a lonely triptych against the big sky. The tide is a mile out and there is nothing.

Then, there is someone else.

'You're doing a fine job there, young man.'

The boy looks around at a stranger who has suddenly appeared behind him. A very thin man with an unkempt greying beard and a battered old anorak.

'Expert kite-flying there, and entertaining your sister too.' He speaks without the local accent; a southerner.

'She's not my sister. My mum's a foster carer.'

'Ah, then what a lovely family you must be. She looks very happy.

1

Hello dear,' he shouts, absurdly, at the pram.

'She can't hear you, she's deaf.'

'Ah. Yes of course.'

They stand for a while, all three looking at the kite as it hovers and dances.

'Turning and turning in the widening gyre, the falcon cannot hear the falconer,' said the man, his words disappearing into the wind, as if they never existed.

'You what?'

'Oh, nothing,' the man smiles, raising his voice again. 'Just half-remembering a poem. *The Second Coming* by Yeats. You'll read it in school one day, no doubt.' He nods to the pram. 'And your mother lets you take her to the beach alone?'

'No, she's just gone to the car to get something. D'you wanna have a go then?' Uncertainly, the boy offers the kite handle.

'No, no, thank you. I'm just keeping watch. Like the proverbial shepherd.'

Up on the promenade the figure of a woman appears. When she sees the man, she begins to run towards them, shouting angrily.

'Well, goodbye then,' says the man. He looks at the baby, the child that is his, and not his, before marching away across the sand almost at a run.

Chapter One

A hundred metres further along, the promenade ends and the clear sand melds into the Blitz Beach, where World War Two rubble was dumped in the 1940s. This stretch of beach from Blundellsands up the coast to Formby is territory at once forgotten, yet steeped in history. The sand reveals its secrets periodically, drawing back to reveal an eighteenth-century shipwreck; a red brick softened by the tide; the tile of a bombed-out bathroom; a Neolithic footprint; an ammonite; the fossil of some dinosaur-like creature. A liminal space where nothing ever happens, and yet where all of human history is stored in its shifting sands. Here is deep time, where everything is connected.

A woman stoops and combs the intertidal zone, as hunter-gatherers have done since prehistoric times, as cockle-mollies did in the eighteenth century. Her skirts are sodden and trailing, and her grey matted hair falls around her face. She stumbles frequently, uneasy on her feet. Over the sea, the setting sun casts glorious shadows on the clouds and the sky roars like purple fire. Only a lone cargo ship easing into the port of Liverpool betrays the modernity of the scene.

She collects razor clams and seaweed, to go with the rabbit she caught earlier. It would be easier to steal from the bins in the golf club car park, but she prefers to stay away from people. Must stay away from people, until They come for her. *Be thou as a stranger on earth.*

In the fading light she steals back to the shelter, lurching over the war rubble and into the dunes, where her diminutive colourless figure is camouflaged by the clumps of tall marram grass, until she reaches the entrance, little more than a crack in the concrete at ground level. She feels safe here. It had once been a childhood hideout, and she had somehow remembered how to come back. In another life she had played here, played house underground, like a foreshadowing of her oubliette. This is where she belongs. She fingers the thread around her neck, to check it is still there, giving a last furtive glance towards the car park as she lowers herself backwards through the crack. Still no message from Them.

As the winter sun disappears below the horizon, her underground fire can just be seen at the shelter entrance. It makes a faint glow that lights up the marram grass fronds, like so many daggers against the sky.

Decades ago, this light would have been the Starfish decoy, drawing German bombers away from the city. Now it has drawn other lights. Police torches.

Thy kingdom come, thy will be done…

Chapter Two

Darren stared into his pint and allowed the comforting pub sounds to wash over him, numbing the questions that plagued his subconscious. Most of the pubs around here were more like nightclubs nowadays, live DJs blasting house music, drinkers in their best clothes ready to taxi it into the city centre later. But The Crown & Anchor remained a resolutely traditional pub, quiet enough that Darren could listen to others' conversations, to distract him from the torments inside his head. It was busier than usual tonight, however, because there was a Liverpool match on. From his table in the corner, Darren joined the other drinkers in looking up to the screen above the bar, where the players were running out onto the pitch, led by Thomas Kuper.

He vaguely tried to imagine bringing Thomas here, and couldn't. He found it difficult to imagine anything in the future now, in this limbo period. He couldn't imagine what he would do with this theology degree, for which he had taken a sabbatical from a perfectly good job he hadn't even been doing for that long. He wasn't really committing to anything, and there was a notion at the fringes of his thoughts, slightly terrifying, that he could easily go on doing this forever.

What was this period of his life, and should he even analyse it? Matt had been dead nine months, and he was with Thomas - or was he? With Justine gone, Thomas was single – but he was not free. They had to hide their relationship, and that somehow made it easier for Darren to assuage his guilt, because he could almost hide their relationship from himself.

Lamb of God

How to move on in life, having glimpsed something other? Maybe enrolling in a theology degree course at the university was the best thing he could have done, or maybe the worst. It was very possible that he was in the process of destroying his career. He had filled his days with a spiritual quest for answers to the ephemeral, the liminal, the indefinable, the barely there. Questions that were either pointless, or the most important questions of all. Perhaps it would have been better to stay with the police, and immerse himself in the brutal mundanity of burglary, affray, fraud… He had wanted to escape reality, but now found himself floating between worlds – the world of intellectual pursuits, and the glamorous world of football. He didn't fit into either; he was on the fringes, the eternal outsider. Fully aware that his natural morosity was taking full advantage of his recent misfortunes, Darren was bathing in it. Thank goodness for Colette and her energy. A drink with his former colleague had become the anchor of his week, an anchor in the reality from which he had thought he wanted to escape.

'Sorry, sorry.'

Rolling into the pub, Colette squeezed his shoulders from behind, slid into her seat, and took a gulp of the white wine he had waiting for her, all in one movement. 'Sorry I'm late. It's been all go today, honest to god.'

She was still in uniform and had been spotted from the bar. 'Aye aye lads, it's the bizzies, quick hide your stash…'

'It's alright lads, I'm off duty. As you were.' Colette wafted her hand and winked at them. Darren felt himself instantly relax, at her friendly touch, the waft of her perfume slightly stale after a long shift.

'Don't tell me,' he said leaning back and smiling, 'New bike theft? Old lady got herself locked out?'

'No, actually,' she said, making a face at his sarcasm. 'It's all happening down the seafront. We've got the Wild Woman Of Blundellsands.'

'The what?'

'Oh, you'll probably read about it in the Echo tomorrow. This woman - she was living in the dunes, catching rabbits, eating seaweed, mussels, god knows what, and cooking them over a fire in one of the World War Two bunkers. Can you imagine? All those mansions and millionaires down there, and then someone living like a cavewoman just a stone's throw away. Anyway, a jogger spotted her fire so they called the police, thought it was kids up to no good.'

'But she can't have been there long, right? Someone would have noticed her – it's not completely deserted around there.'

'No, exactly, she must have arrived there recently.'

'Well, what does she say?'

'That's just it, she doesn't say anything. She's mute. We've got her in Aintree Psychiatric Ward at the moment. I don't think there's ever been a homeless person in Blundellsands.'

'What's her health like?'

'She's white as a sheet, looks like a ghost. Skeleton thin, cuts and bruises, and apparently severe osteoporosis and vitamin D deficiency. And obviously her state of mind is highly agitated, doesn't know what's going on.'

'Sounds like the beginnings of a mystery,' said Darren. 'I almost wish I was back on the case.'

'Let's see how I get on without you. What did you always teach me?' She counted on her fingers. 'One. There are no coincidences. Two. Use Occam's Razor. The simplest explanation is usually the answer. Right? Anyway, how are you? How's that sabbatical coming along?'

Darren nodded, as convincingly as he could. 'It's alright, yeah. I've read more books in the last three months than I have in the last ten years.'

'But books about religion? After your childhood, I would

have thought religion would be the last thing you'd study.'

'I know, yeah. It was embarrassing, in a way, to announce it to everyone at work. It would be one thing to go off and do a degree in Criminology or Law, but what policeman studies Theology? The truth is that it's been a sort of therapy, you know, to study religion from another angle, from the outside.'

Darren was only half-lying. Colette knew about his strict religious upbringing within a cult, and there was something cathartic about considering other aspects of religion, but she didn't know the real reason why he was studying Theology. He wasn't sure he understood it himself. Colette had been there with him throughout the cases of the past eighteen months, but she had only seen one side. She hadn't seen what he had seen. Or what he thought he had seen.

'I must admit it took me a while to get me head around it, Darren. But I suppose religion is bound up with so much of world history, politics, culture… for better or worse.'

'Usually worse.'

'So, it's just another way of studying other subjects, that makes sense,' she nodded. 'I miss you, you know. We were a good team.'

'I miss you too. I feel even more of an impostor as a student than I did as a detective.'

'Impostor syndrome is the sign of someone who's good at what they do. Anyway, what about romance? Anyone new yet?'

Darren shook his head and smiled. 'No, not yet. I'm not ready.'

With perfect timing, there was a roar from the bar as Liverpool scored - Thomas taking a penalty. Darren and Colette turned their heads to join the throng watching as Thomas took his victory run towards the Kop and fell to his knees, arms outstretched to receive the adulation of the crowd, joined by other members of the team who jumped on him to share the moment.

The inevitable chant of 'Super Kuper,' to the familiar ABBA

melody, began in the stadium crowd and the drinkers joined in, a couple of the more drunk patrons running around the pub with arms outstretched.

'Kuper's on fire at the moment, isn't he? He's really become one of Liverpool's own,' said Colette, turning back to Darren.

He hated lying to her. Was it really lying? If he and Thomas weren't even in a real relationship? A part of him couldn't wait to text Thomas afterwards and congratulate him, wait to see if he was invited over, decide if he would accept the invitation. And another part of him wished it would all just go away.

Colette's phone buzzed. 'Sorry – I'd better check this. Oh… it looks as if our Wild Woman is talking! I'd better get down to the hospital. Sorry, Darren.' She started to get up.

'No worries,' he said. 'Listen, just one thing that I thought of. If you don't mind. You said it might be in the Echo tomorrow?'

'Yeah…'

'I would try and keep it out of the press for now. This woman could be running from someone – domestic violence or whatever. You don't want to compromise the case.'

'Ok, boss. You just can't keep away from the job, can you?'

She smiled and winked at him as she backed out of the double doors.

That evening, Darren lay in bed alone, scrolling through his phone. Sleep never came easy, but it was impossible to relax in this ridiculous, childish situation. Liverpool had won 2-0, with Thomas scoring one goal and setting up the other. He would be home by now, would have checked on Alfie, dismissed the babysitter…

Darren typed out a text, his thumb hovering over the send button. He saw the ellipsis that showed Thomas was writing to him at the same time... but the message never came, so he didn't send his either. Frustrated, feeling like a teenager, he texted Colette instead.

'Nice to see you tonight mate. What did the Wild Woman say then?'

'Not much. Just the same thing, over and over again.'

'Go on then.'

'I was buried with Christ. And now I am risen.'

'Ah. Nutter?'

'Probably. Maybe you could ask that nun of yours, Helen.'

Chapter Three

'Behold the Lamb of God, which taketh away the sin of the world.' John 1.29. 'The suffering and death of Jesus is at the centre of Christian faith. When you think about it, it's an incredibly brutal concept. Almost too brutal to contemplate. A son begging his father to spare him from torture and death. So, is Christianity nothing more than a death cult?'

Helen often marvelled at her new way of teaching; in fact, her whole new way of thinking about religion. Deaconess Margaret would be horrified at this almost blasphemous provocation. But using heretical shock-tactics seemed to get better results from her students; it captured their attention. She didn't want them to be afraid to think, and to express their thoughts, out of respect for her beliefs. When she had dressed as a nun her severe attire had been a novelty, but she now realised it had stifled the students. Now that she dressed like them - indeed, even more unconventionally than them in her heavy metal t-shirts, gothic make-up and loose black hair - they felt relaxed enough to express alternative viewpoints.

'Some people struggle with the idea of a God that required such a violent sacrifice. But is it God who needed the sacrifice, or us? Humans have always had a need for sacrifice. Jesus' sacrifice was prefigured by Leviticus, and Old Testament sacrifice was prefigured by the Vestal Virgins, by Neolithic bog burials. The Aztecs believed that human sacrifice was necessary to feed the sun and maintain the harmony of the universe, and that they were the people chosen to perform this duty.'

She flashed up a series of images on the projector screen, ending with a Rubens painting of the crucifixion.

'The anthropologist René Girard argued that humanity is fundamentally violent, and the ritual of violent sacrifice allows us to contain this violence, by offloading the blame for our sins onto an outsider, a scapegoat. The Lamb of God. We can only form groups by forming those groups *against* someone. Some of the earliest evidence for human sacrifice dates from 6000 BCE, among the Mesopotamians. A means of exchange throughout history between a community and its god or gods. The beauty of Christianity is that Jesus made the ultimate sacrifice – the sacrifice to end all sacrifices, that atoned for all of the sins of humanity in one go, ending the need for further violence.'

And I should know more than anyone about sacrifice, thought Helen. *I was complicit in my own subjugation. Ten years in a convent.* And then she realised that she was comparing herself to Jesus, and laughed at herself and loathed herself.

'So, if religion is a way of controlling humanity's violence, what happens now that religion is in decline? There is plenty of scapegoating in the modern world – we could even argue that there is more. Perhaps the rise of modern scapegoating is linked to the decline of religion. Or maybe it's just the consequences of social media. However, these ancient narratives persist. What does that mean for Christianity?'

A student put up his hand. 'But if it's humans that required the sacrifice, isn't the ultimate conclusion that the God part is just a story? Some guy called Jesus might have been crucified, sure, but...'

Helen nodded. 'Now that's a question for another time. We're going to look at the evidence for the historical Jesus in our next lecture. I'll just ask this for now. What's the difference between belief and truth?'

'Truth… is fact. Truth is reality,' offered the student.

'But what is reality? I'm being a little facetious here, but do you get my point? Truth is only that which conjures itself into being. If we believe this happened, and use that belief to govern our actions, our values, then does it make any difference whether it actually happened or not? The world is simply an infinite number of alternative histories playing out in real time. They are however we interpret them to be. And the Bible is what we interpret it to be. It's only a small selection of ancient writings; any number of alternative texts could have made the cut.'

As the students filed out, turning phones on and chatting, Helen smiled and waved at Darren, who was waiting in his seat to speak to her.

'Hello Darren! It's still so strange to see you in my lectures, taking notes. I haven't quite got used to you yet. It's rather unnerving. The first time you came in here, I was something of a suspect.'

'I'm the one who's unnerved. I'm totally out of my comfort zone here with all these nerds and boffins. Sorry. Students. I'm getting the hang of it though. Have you got time for a coffee? It's my turn to invite you.'

They walked along Hope Street, heading for their favourite student café. Rain had been intermittent all day and the windows of the packed café were fogged, obscuring their view of the cathedrals at each end of the street. The modernist spikes of the Metropolitan cathedral at one end, the gothic tower of the Anglican, high above St James' Mount, at the other. Catholic and Protestant together in the same vista.

Darren brought their coffees over to Helen's window table, eyeing the groups of animated youths, and the lone essay-writers on laptops.

'I still don't feel like I belong here.'

'Oh, neither do I, and I've been here more than ten years. Perhaps you and I are both destined to not belong anywhere.'

They swirled their coffees, both momentarily lost in semi-shared memories. Helen licked the chocolate powder from her spoon.

'Are you missing the police?'

'Yes and no. I don't miss the management. I wasn't cut out for all that. I'm the definition of over-promoted. It felt as if I'd hardly been out of uniform five minutes before I was Detective Inspector. And it was stressful. But then… I see Colette once a week for a pint, and I can't help wondering what they're all up to. So, I miss the buzz of it, yeah.'

'It must be frustrating. I imagine she can't tell you all that much.'

'No, exactly, but since we're mates, she gives me little snatches. Actually, I saw Colette last night, and we've got a question for you.'

'That sounds ominous. We know what happened last time you came to me with a religious puzzle. Go on.'

'So, they found a woman living wild in the sand dunes. Hard to believe actually.'

Helen nodded. 'The Wild Woman of Blundellsands.'

'You know about it?'

'Yes, it was in the Echo this morning.'

Darren groaned. 'I told Colette to keep that quiet.'

'Why?'

'In case she escaped from somewhere, or someone. Because according to the doctors she hadn't been living outside for long. In fact, they think from her lack of vitamin D she had been indoors for a long time. Anyway, she started talking, but it's all muttering and nonsense. All they can make out is "I was buried with Christ. I was buried with Christ, and now I am risen." Does that mean anything to you?'

Helen shrugged, and looked around for inspiration. 'Well, the first thing that springs to mind is baptism. Baptism is supposed to be like a funeral. A burial of your old self. *We were therefore buried with him through baptism into death, in order that, just as Christ was raised from the dead through the glory of the father, we too may live a new life.* So, you are dead to sin, alive to God. It is a rather morbid way of looking at baptism, I admit. But let's face it, the Bible is pretty morbid.'

'So, she could have had some sort of religious epiphany or awakening and then...' Darren looked into space, trying to imagine scenarios. 'No, it doesn't really help.'

'She could be schizophrenic. A psychiatric case.'

'Oh, she's definitely a psychiatric case. But high functioning, if she knew how to survive in the wild.'

'It does remind me of something else actually,' said Helen, tapping the table as she searched for an idea just out of reach. 'Simply because you mentioned that she might have been indoors for a long time. It's a little obscure though. Anchoresses. Or anchorites - they could be men too.'

'Anchoress?'

'It's a very extreme version of the hermetic life. A nun or monk, or a lay person actually, who would allow themselves to be literally walled in for the rest of their lives. A special chamber would be built into the walls of the church, with no door. They would go through a ceremony that was effectively a funeral, and often they would dig their own grave, then contemplate that open grave for the rest of their lives. A living dead person. Buried alive, you know.'

'But that wasn't actually a thing though.'

'Oh, it was. In medieval times. It wasn't common, but it was a thing. There's plenty of written evidence, and there are still some anchorholds remaining, attached to medieval churches. They were terribly small.'

'Who would do that?'

'Not many. But I suppose we have to remember that medieval life was often so hard as to be unbearable. Occasionally it was an escape from impending forced marriage. And it was also a perverse sort of exhibitionism, really. Anchorites were venerated as saints. You got to be a martyr, yet stay alive to bask in your glory. A living saint. They also had servants, visitors, everything taken care of for them. Anyway, it's rather obscure. A very esoteric aspect of Christian mysticism, which pretty much died out with the Reformation. I suspect there were far more people interested in writing manuals for anchoresses than willing victims.'

'Willing victims….' Darren thought for a moment. 'So there is evidence that this really happened? A sort of Stockholm syndrome with God as your captor?'

'With the local bishop as your captor. There was great prestige in having an anchorite or anchoress attached to your church, so bishops were all for it.'

'Like having a holy relic.'

'Exactly, it was supposed to be completely voluntary. But you do wonder about coercion. There's an anchorhold near here actually, attached to a church in Lunt. And there are so many medieval texts to read on the subject. Actually,' she tapped the table again. 'It might be an interesting dissertation topic. It's quite prescient, with all this post-feminism stuff. And isolation is a major theme of modern life. These days there are so many different types of isolation, alienation. In some ways we are more connected than ever, in others we have never felt more alone.'

'Perhaps all those internet personalities are like modern anchorites; heroes and yet without any meaningful human connection.'

They talked for a while longer, and Helen jotted him a reading list. He looked around him at the groups of students and academics, and realised that he was one of them, that he too was having an academic discussion, and that he enjoyed it. There was something so indulgent about all this, spending time thinking about obscure medieval texts, ephemeral ideas, while the world turned about him. He felt that time had slowed down and given him space to think. It made him feel thrilled and guilty at the same time. As if reading his mind, Helen stopped scribbling down her list, reached across the table and put her hand over his.

'Darren. It's ok. You are allowed to take time off to think. Especially after everything you have been through. Imagine if nobody ever stopped to think about these things. There would be no progress in any academic subject. You'd be entitled to go on holiday for a year, after all that's happened, not to mention everything you've achieved. But you're not on holiday, you're doing a university degree. It has intrinsic value, and also practical value. So just enjoy it.'

'I do enjoy it. I do. Thanks.'

She tore the reading list she had jotted for him out of her notebook and pushed it across the table emphatically.

'And now, on to more important matters. Are you coming to Mikko's birthday party on Saturday?'

'Mikko? Is he here?'

'He's arriving tomorrow. Been on tour the past three months.'

Darren winced at himself again. So wrapped up in himself as usual, he hadn't thought to ask Helen about her life.

'Then surely you'll want to be just the two of you.'

'Oh no, there's plenty of time for that. I want… well, it would be nice if he felt at home here. Is that terribly manipulative of me? And I want him to think I have friends. After all, I am one of those nerds of which you speak so disparagingly.'

'You do have friends! Including me. Alright then. Where's the party?'

'The Black Dog. I haven't been there before, but it's a rock and metal pub apparently, so I booked some tables. And why don't you bring Thomas?'

'Actually, that bar is such a dive it's one of the few places in Liverpool where Thomas might not get hassled.'

'Perfect. Well, I must get to the departmental meeting.'

'I'll go home and start on that essay then.'

'Now I hope you're not expecting any special treatment just because we are friends,' she said as she stood up to put on her raincoat. 'I will say this though. Don't forget to read the footnotes. Sometimes the meanings are in the margins. Hiding in plain sight. In front of your eyes, yet you don't think to look.'

'You make it sound like detective work.'

'Exactly!'

Chapter Four

That afternoon he sat at the kitchen table in his narrow-terraced house, looking out to the tiny garden which he still hadn't got round to doing. It was paved in grey concrete slabs, between which rogue weeds sprouted, dotted this time of year with bright yellow dandelions and buttercups. Slivers of optimism through the grey. The only garden furniture was a rusting barbecue that he hadn't touched since before Matt died. Over the back wall he could see the blue and yellow cranes of the docks. Darren always felt grounded by those cranes. They calmed him, at the same time as the hovering seagulls unnerved him, harbingers of something. The long evening stretched ahead with not even the possibility of company, since Thomas was at an away match. And it was partly a relief to know not to expect his call.

Darren surveyed the books he had collected from the library based on Helen's reading list. Again, he felt that excitement tinged with guilt, and the sheer indulgence of it – here was a mystery that might be purely intellectual. *The Ancrene Riwle*, with its irresistible old-English spelling – an anonymous manual for female anchoresses written in the thirteenth century. *The Revelations of Divine Love*, a medieval book of Christian mystical devotions, written by a woman called Julian of Norwich who was herself an anchoress. *The Scale of Perfection*, another manual for women written by a man, Walter Hilton, who in the fourteenth century spent ninety-three chapters addressing an anchoress on how to extirpate the 'foul image of sin' from her soul.

Lamb of God

These books were so enticing, in a strange, arcane way, in their utter foreignness. This time last year he would have been reading police reports. Darren tried to analyse the texts the way he had been taught by Helen. It was a different sort of analysis from detective work. Both techniques were forms of critical analysis - he was required to make judgements - but here morality came into it somehow differently.

Helen was right, it really had been a thing. By the thirteenth century there were two hundred of them recorded in England. These anchoresses – for women outnumbered men in the practice by three to one, the men preferring to be hermits which at least allowed them physical freedom – were like supernuns. The ultimate nuns, the cloistered life taken to its logical conclusion. He smiled at the thought that Mikko would have said they were metal. An anchoress would literally go through her own burial ceremony. The liturgy for her initiation ceremony was essentially a funeral liturgy, as it was deemed she was dying to the world and to herself. She was spoken of as already dead, already with God in Heaven. Her cell was called her 'burial chamber', and, dressed in a shroud, she was directed to sing a verse from Psalm 132: "*This is my resting place forever, here shall I dwell for I have chosen it.*" The ceremony, attended by family, friends and benefactors, would end with the doorway to her cell being forever cemented over. Only a slit would be left, for food and other necessities to be passed to her, and waste products to be passed out. Often, she would dig her own grave inside the cell, for her to contemplate every day.

As he read, Darren realised why these texts were so enticing. Firstly, because they were real texts; unlike fantastical grimoires and mythologies, these were manuals by which real people lived real lives. But it wasn't just that. It was because they were a little sexual, almost fetishistic. There was a prurience to it all, that he felt even as he was repulsed. Some of the details were gloriously sordid; instructions on personal touch, personal hygiene, even rules for private thoughts. And his guilty interest in it all, the slight glee of it, his affinity somewhere deep inside with the author, made him feel personally implicated.

He had always found it weird that nuns literally married God, but this went even further, the idea being that the anchoress would have a full-on sensual experience of Heaven. Some of the texts had titles like The Prickynge of Love (Stimulus Amoris) and The Fire of Love (Incendium Amoris). In the Ancrene Riwle, God informed the anchoress to 'show your face to me, and no other. I am not a bold lover. I will embrace my spouse only in a retired place.' And the anchoress was told that after the kiss of peace in the Mass, she would 'forget the world, be completely out of the body, and with burning love embrace your Beloved who has come down from Heaven to your heart's bower, and hold him fast until He has granted you all that you ask.' It was an almost orgasmic description of spirituality.

To Darren it seemed like a sort of perversion. He couldn't help but allow his curiosity to be stirred by the carnal squalor of it. The instructions for an anchoress' daily living were detailed to the point of extreme mundanity, such was the level of control these rule-writers insisted on exerting over an imprisoned woman's life. The level of control made him think of sadomasochism, of those absurd rules in Fifty Shades of Grey. The anchoress was instructed to revel in her own stench: 'On Mount Calvary, where Our Lord hung on the cross, was the place of execution where decaying bodies often lay unburied in great stench, and He, as He hung there, had their stench fill His nostrils, in the midst of all his other suffering.'

The anchoress was not allowed to commit self-harm, for that would be vanity. But she must shave her head four times a year, and keep her hands dirty – so she could not admire their beauty – by scraping up earth every day from the grave in which she would eventually rot.

There seemed no doubt, however, that women were not

forced into this way of life. They chose it voluntarily, and were then tested rigorously by bishops for their suitability for the role, since failure would bring disrepute to the church, and cause the anchoress's certain descent into Hell. Willing victims.

Darren's noticeboard leaned against the wall at the edge of the table. The dreaded corkboard, Matt had used to call it, when it had been overflowing with the minutiae of Darren's criminal cases – maps and Post-Its and print-outs of spreadsheets scrawled with highlighter pen and question marks. Now it was empty apart from an A4 sheet with his university course timetable, and a cluster of unused pins. He wrote the word 'anchoress' on a Post-It and stuck it in the centre of the board. A new project.

Chapter Five

'Does Sister Helen know how to throw a party or what?'

'Since it's your birthday I will allow you to call me that. I'm sorry, Mikko, this isn't really what I imagined for your party. I don't know what I imagined. I've never actually organised a party.'

Mikko and Helen sat side by side at a table in the Black Dog, in a raised area at the back which allowed them to survey the whole bar. The Black Dog was a traditional pub which had been commandeered at some point as rock-and-metal-themed, and so the traditional oak-panelled walls were plastered with vintage festival posters, and while the floor was all threadbare patterned carpet, the ceiling was hung with a motley collection of animal skulls and metal memorabilia. Instead of the usual Liverpool bar soundtrack of house music, there was a heavy metal jukebox, and they could hear the sounds of Iron Maiden loud and clear, since the bar was three-quarters empty despite it being Saturday night.

'I didn't need a party, I love being here with you in this city. And I love that you got some choir nerds and theology lecturers to go to a metal pub.'

'I'm not sure if they are enjoying themselves - look.' She nudged him.

Three women from Helen's church choir sipped gin-and-tonics nervously at a table nearby, and she could tell from their facial expressions that they were evaluating the music, and were not convinced. At the bar, two of Helen's university colleagues, with almost matching brown leather satchels and corduroys, nursed pints of lager.

'I'm only disappointed you didn't bring any nuns.'

Helen still struggled with public displays of affection, and she tried to relax into the feeling of his arm around her shoulder, instead of being embarrassed. She traced the scrawlings on the worn wooden table; drunken graffiti probably decades old, key carvings, glass rings. And then she traced the spindly tattoos on his fingers.

'Maybe you wanted to go home and rest after your tour.'

'It's March. Norway is still dark right now. Anyway, I'm starting to feel at home right here. Hey look, there's Darren and Thomas. That will inject some glamour into proceedings.'

They certainly did make a handsome couple as they squeezed into the chairs opposite; with chiselled features, designer stubble, designer shirts and brand-new trainers. Darren had temporarily given up his police salary, but it was a struggle for him to give up his guilty pleasure of the latest colourful Nikes. They both shook hands with Mikko to wish him happy birthday, and then there was a moment of awkward silence before Darren said, echoing Mikko:

'Helen, you really know how to throw a party.'

As they laughed, ice broken, Helen reddened. Only a year ago, if anyone had made fun of her she would have been mortified, and possibly cried about it later. Now she felt a warm glow at the thought of having friends who knew her well enough to tease her.

Mikko and Thomas went to the bar. She and Darren watched them affectionately; such an incongruous pair, the footballer over a head taller than the guitarist. Thomas was muscular and perfectly groomed, smartly dressed in expensive clothes, while Mikko was thin as a girl and almost comically scruffy.

'What on earth are they talking about, do you think?' said Darren.

Darren couldn't help but like Mikko. He couldn't decide if the Norwegian was the most awkward or the most laid-back person he had ever met, but he was certainly a mass of contradictions. He had a knack of cutting to the very heart of the matter with some inane or foul-mouthed remark, and while he professed to be a

Satan worshipper, he had the kindest heart of any of them.

'Who knows,' smiled Helen. 'Mikko seems to know how to talk to anyone, even a severe Swiss footballer. How's Thomas doing?'

'Ok. It's been - what? Six months since Justine died. He's not really grieving for himself, more for Alfie and Val. His marriage to Justine had been over to all intents and purposes for a long time – it was just keeping up appearances by then. And then when it transpired what she'd done…'

They looked at each other. Because what had she done? No-one would ever know if behind Justine's vacant blue eyes there had been something unimaginably dark. But if there was, she hadn't inherited it from her own mother, Val, but from Thomas' grandmother. They both shuddered, knowing the other was thinking about that sinister old woman they had met in Switzerland.

'Val's looking after Alfie tonight, actually,' said Darren.

'Is she?' Helen's eyes widened, and she tried to check her involuntary grimace. Thomas Kuper's mother-in-law was the wife of notorious crime boss Max Killy, and when the footballer had married their beautiful daughter Justine, he had unwittingly married into a dangerous situation.

'I know, yeah. It comes to something when he would trust a gangland murderer's wife, who's done multiple sentences for perjury, more than he'd trust his own family.'

'Gosh yes, that Kuper grandmother. She was terrifying. But who'd have thought.'

'They never found Justine's body, you know. Sometimes I look at that baby Alfie, and I see his mother's eyes. And it gives me the creeps, to be honest.'

Mikko and Thomas still hadn't returned with drinks, as they had drawn quite a crowd over at the bar. Mikko was a celebrity in a heavy metal pub, and Thomas one of the most famous people in Liverpool. Darren and Helen watched them as they sheepishly posed for selfies with delighted drinkers.

'Is he going to come out?' asked Helen. 'It's sort of an open secret, isn't it?'

'No, not yet. Actually, it isn't – I mean, it is a secret. You're one of the few people who know. He will though – he told me he's planning to do it soon. I don't know, it's to do with sponsorship and whatnot. And some of the fans are dead homophobic. Not here, but in some places abroad, and on social media, you know. Hard to believe in this day and age, but it's scary for him. I know how he feels, it took me long enough to come out to the police. Between you and me, he's asked for a transfer abroad. There's a lot of bad memories here.'

'Oh. How do you feel about that?'

Darren looked at her and paused for a moment, and his voice cracked a little.

'He asked me to go with him. But – it's still not that long since Matt… and anyway I belong here. Can you see me, a kept man in some foreign city?'

Helen smiled sympathetically. 'I can't tell you what to do, Darren. But I will say this. That night when I stood outside Mikko's hotel room, I was on a precipice. The choice before me was clear: either a chance at happiness, or a life of duty and guilt. Duty and guilt that could easily have been misplaced. That *were* misplaced. I have no regrets.'

Darren smiled at her. 'You shagged a guitarist. It's not the same as moving your life half-way round the world.'

'Darren! I broke all my vows!'

'I'm only messing.'

'I know. I'm just saying – doors not opened, passages not taken, that sort of thing.'

Darren nodded, and they clinked glasses amiably, then both smiled as the music was suddenly turned up and a cheer rose from the bar.

'I presume that's a Total Depravity song?' said Darren. 'I think I recognise Mikko's voice.'

'It is indeed,' nodded Helen. 'This one is called Angel's Entrails, unfortunately.'

They were silent for a moment. Darren was staring into his pint, and Helen eventually reached across the table and touched his finger lightly.

'I know exactly how you're feeling. You're feeling that to make the move with Thomas would be to disturb the universe irreparably, and yet at the same time to make yourself disappear. Allow the universe to swallow you up. It's making you dizzy, to contemplate the entropy of it.'

'Nail on the head. So, I take it you're feeling something similar?'

She looked over to the bar, from where Mikko and Thomas were finally returning with their drinks.

'Yes, I do feel sort of on the edge of a cliff. In a good way, you know.'

Helen's choir friends had drawn an admirer of their own; or rather, they were admiring someone. The three women, faces shining upwards, were in thrall to an extraordinarily handsome man who was standing at their table handing them each a leaflet. He had shoulder length golden-brown hair and wore a striped cheesecloth kaftan-style cardigan over a yellow t-shirt. The women seemed delighted with their leaflets, turning them over and over as he explained something to them with grand gestures and flourishing hand movements.

'Right, let's take bets,' said Darren, leaning in conspiratorially. 'Which one of them is going to pull him?'

'None of them,' said Helen, looking over disconcertedly. 'I know that man from somewhere, he looks familiar.'

Their view was blocked by Mikko and Thomas returning with the drinks.

'Sorry we took so long, we had to deal with our adoring fans over there.' Mikko gestured to the bar, where every face was turned to its phone, every thumb furiously recording the celebrity encounter for the world to see. As he handed out the glasses, Mikko was almost knocked over by the choir girls who huddled around Helen excitedly.

'Helen, you won't believe it. We have to do this. We've been invited to sing at a festival, look! Our choir!'

They thrust a leaflet at Helen, and she peered at it before nodding in recognition. 'Oh, it's the Guardians Of Truth. They are creationists, unfortunately.' She rolled her eyes at Darren, showing him the leaflet. 'That's how I recognise him. They run a youth festival every year just outside Manchester – it's the biggest Christian music festival in the UK. Look, Mikko, maybe you could play there too.'

Mikko took the leaflet and read aloud, '*Would you and your band like to minister Jesus in the UK*? Fuck no.'

'I think you'd be struck down by a thunderbolt from Heaven the moment you set foot in the place,' said Darren.

'*Our music is for the Jesus lovers AND the Jesus haters,*' Mikko continued to read. 'I wonder which I am.' He stuck up his middle finger to reveal an inverted cross.

Helen rolled her eyes again, and Mikko mocked her. 'I know. Could I be any more offensive? But.' He tapped the leaflet. 'It says here they have Sporn as their headliner. Rex Molina. Now that is a game changer.'

'Even I've heard of Sporn,' said Darren. 'Eighties thrash metal, right?'

'You are learning, man. Exactly. Original Bay Area thrash. They were huge – should have been bigger than Metallica. But their singer Rex Molina became a born-again Christian about fifteen years ago, and left the band to become a preacher. Pastor Rex. He became huge in America. And then out of the blue he rejoined Sporn last year, making them the biggest Christian metal band in the world. Hey dude,' he called to the handsome man, who was pinning a poster on the wall nearby. 'Do you really have Sporn?'

The man looked around and smiled. 'We do. You're Mikko from

Total Depravity, correct? I'm a big fan.' He came over and shook the disarmed Mikko's hand. 'I'm Jared Case, director of Truth Fest. We would be honoured if you played, actually. It would bring in a new crowd – we're somewhat preaching to the converted at the moment, as you can imagine. There's plenty of time to change the line-up, and in fact it would give us some great publicity to announce a new band. It would certainly court controversy, and all publicity is good publicity, isn't that what they say?'

'So can we, can we?' The choir girls were almost jumping up and down.

Incredulous, irritated, Helen said, 'The Angel of Liverpool choir can sing if Total Depravity play too.'

'How about this' said Mikko, slapping the table, 'Total Depravity will play if you agree to come on tour with me this summer. Band wife. And it's my birthday so you have to say yes.'

Lips tight, Helen agreed.

The evening continued, far more animated now as the bar filled up and the drinks flowed. Helen tried not to be bad-tempered. On what level of irony would they be attending this festival? It didn't make sense. What was Mikko thinking? He must have known she wouldn't find this funny. Maybe she didn't know him as well as she had thought.

'That negotiation didn't go the way you wanted, did it?' said Mikko eventually. 'Come on, it will be fun.'

'I don't think it's funny at all. Anyway, surely the rest of your band won't agree to play at a Christian festival? It's insane. You are supposed to be official Satanists.'

'Oh, they will do it for sure, Knut will think this is the biggest piss-take.'

'It is. And the joke is on who?'

'Oh, fuck it. This is the age of irresponsibility, I'm thirty-two today. Next year is my Jesus year.'

'Jesus year?' asked Thomas.

'Yeah, thirty-three. It's the age Jesus was crucified. It's the age when you're supposed to get serious about life. After that it's all over. How old are you then, Thomas?'

'Fortunately, I am twenty-eight. Although that's old in footballer years.'

'What about you Darren? You are looking worried.'

'I'm thirty-three.'

'So am I,' said Helen.

'Oh shit…'

Chapter Six

Tyres race over the dirt track, bump over rogue stones and into miniature ditches. The boys stand up off their seats and pedal hard, letting their blazers and ties flap behind them. The exhilaration of after-school freedom is heightened by their mission, this long-planned transgression. Because they have gone off-road. Only for a few minutes, and only a few hundred metres from their house, but the copse has mythologised in their minds into a place of fear and magic. At morning break today, they finally made their pact to go in, they dared each other, and the shared secret now holds more power than the act itself.

Sniggery Woods. A sniggery is an eel pond, and there were lots around here, back in the day. But the boys don't know that. The mysterious word is both absurd and terrifying; a joke, or a witch; comedy or sorcery. To snigger is to half-suppress a secret laugh. But there is also something comically sinister about it. Sniggery Woods is less a forest than a copse; a stubborn little patch of woodland that clings to its place in the fields - a link to ancient times before the land was cleared. Tangles of bramble and nettle layer the floor, while gnarled branches of spindly trees, some long dead, twist up stark against the sky. A copse can only be ancient, must always hold mystery and secrets. A connection with deep time, an anchor with the past. Stabilising the land in history, like stitching. If there are local legends about the copse, the boys don't need them; they have invented their own.

The dirt track is just wide enough for three bikes, but they instinctively fall into single file, afraid to veer into one of the ditches

31

that line each side. Ditches where they have seen the holes that promise water voles, but never the creatures themselves. Water voles and eels – so seldom spotted that there is no hope or expectation of a sighting, but still a comfort to know they must be there. Traces, another reality, the possibility of a miracle one day. Just knowing they exist is something.

The boys arrive parallel with the copse now, fifty metres away across the field, and lay down their bikes. The track is a public bridleway, but the fields are private farmland. They jump over the ditch, teetering comically on its far side, and then they instinctively duck down, ready to run.

'Who's going first?'

'Go-ed then!'

'Now!'

They run as if dodging bullets, laughing at themselves, their trainers making footprints in the ploughed soil. They hurdle over the wooden stile and then only the woods are ahead of them. At once less and more frightening than before. They hope for something that will justify their fears, that will make a story, know now that they will find something. It doesn't matter if there's nothing there, they will hear a twig snap, see three ravens, a strangely-shaped tree, and it will be enough to sustain their myth.

It has been a dry March, and unseasonably warm. Usually the track would have been riddled with puddles, the ditches would have been streams, parts of the fields flooded. Their trainers would have been caked in wet mud by now. But instead everything is dry and cracked.

A carpet of bluebells has sprung up, and a light green spring foliage is beginning to cover the trees, but the boys can already see that the wood is small, they can clearly make out the fields on other side, and they fear disappointment, each preparing individually to make something happen. But there is no need.

In the centre of the copse is a real sniggery; in fact, the trees were a mere curtain for it. But there are no eels now. The fields have drained the soil around, leeching half its depth into the ground centuries ago. And the unusual dry spell has parched the rest, so that its contents are revealed.

'Is that a skull?'

'Shut up.'

'It is, it fuckin' is.'

'Oh, my fuckin' god, there's another one!'

The sniggery bed is a bone yard. A heap of refuse sacks from which bodies have escaped. Cracked ribs have torn through black PVC; the cruel domestic indignity of the bin bag a stark contrast with the ancient majesty of a tomb. The skeletons are not scattered throughout the pond bed, but rather form a pile that has toppled and spread slightly. Here a matrix of rugged vertebrae, there a smooth scapula, a half-skull, a hip bone; a jigsaw puzzle of bodies disturbed in the throes of some immutable, undefined activity. Grinning skulls in the tangle give the scene a black comedic feel, a Day of the Dead ensemble piece.

The boys stare open-mouthed at the cartoon gruesomeness before them. This is every horror film they have never been allowed to watch. At the snap of a twig somewhere, their momentary, morbid childish glee is quickly subsumed by the possibility of real danger, not just supernatural, and they are jolted into action. They take one last look at this giant muddy open casket, then peel their eyes away and begin to run.

Chapter Seven

Darren and Colette were back in the pub on Wednesday evening, at their usual table.

'Did you hear about the bones in Sniggery Wood then?' asked Colette.

'No... I've had my head in books all week, not even read the news. I thought I saw a police cordon when I was driving past Dibb Lane the other day though... what happened?'

'Some lads were playing in the woods - they're dead spooky those woods, I remember me and me mates used to dare each other to go in when we were their age. Anyway, there's a pond in there, and it dried up to reveal human skeletons. I mean, we're talking loads of skeletons - they counted twenty.'

'Oh my god. That's mad. So that's a huge investigation - is DCI McGregor doing it?'

'No. It's not actually such a big investigation. Not for the police anyway. We had a forensic archaeologist on site and she identified at least a few of the bones as centuries old. So it looks like it might be an old burial site, maybe a family plot. They've taken it all to the university labs - there's heavy rain forecast this week so they wanted to clear them. It will be exciting for the students, not so exciting for us. It's dead cool though. I always thought those woods were haunted.'

'But that's weird. People do go in there - it's a dog-walkers' place. And it can't be the first time that pond has drained.'

'Apparently it might be. Something to do with the new housing estate in Ince affecting the soil drainage.'

Darren was quiet.

'I know what you're thinking,' said Colette. 'The Wild Woman. There are no coincidences. But I don't see how they can be connected. She can't have put them there herself. And the beach is almost a mile from there.'

'Still. You've got to follow this up, Colette.'

'Of course I will! I'm not completely useless, you know. Is someone missing police work by any chance?'

'No, not really. I'm just… how are you getting on with the wild woman's history, anyway?'

'You know I'm not really supposed to talk to you about the case.'

'But you were ok to talk to the press though.'

'That wasn't me! It was dog-walkers down the beach, they saw us taking her away. Alright, the fact is we haven't made any progress yet. She's in good health – apart from a gash down her side that got infected.'

'How did she get that? Does it look like a struggle? Made by a weapon?'

'Hard to say. Something rusty – that's why it got infected. Other than that, she's fine, eating and so on, but still not speaking much. Less agitated than she was before. We're on Missing Persons, but you know how many of them there are every year. And who knows how far and wide to cast the net.'

'I suggest – if you don't mind – you keep the search very local for now. Go back as far as you like, thirty or forty years if need be, go back to her childhood even – but keep it to Blundellsands and Crosby. That should narrow things down.'

'Why?'

'Because I reckon she's local. Think about it. What was she doing in the sand dunes? You don't just pass through Blundellsands. You don't just end up there by mistake. It's a dead-end. There's one way in and one way out, and it's off the beaten track. Firstly, I think she's been in the area the whole time. Secondly, I think she went to the dunes because she remembered what was there. The World War Two bunkers – a hiding place underground. Maybe she never wanted to escape from wherever she had been hiding before.'

'Ok Detective-Inspector-Darren-Swift who's definitely not missing the police force. So, you haven't given this any thought at all, have you?'

Darren realised, for the first time, that he had given it a lot of thought. This was the first time he had voiced his thoughts, even to himself. He wondered if he was getting his university work confused with this. Conflating, inventing a narrative.

Later that evening, he did an online search and looked up the Sniggery Skeletons, as the press was calling them, and sure enough, there was an item on the local television news. A reporter was interviewing a fairly gleeful archaeologist, a Dr. Amber Rees.

'This is a fabulously exciting discovery and we can't wait to return these skeletons' identities to them and fill in a missing part of history.'

Darren remembered his first television interview, on a windswept Crosby beach at the first murder scene of his career. That was the day he had first met Helen. He didn't even envy the flair of Amber Rees, because he knew that no amount of media training would ever make him less than awkward on camera. This woman was all confident, animated expressions, slightly teasing the viewer, conversational yet superior as she imparted her knowledge.

As he watched, his phone buzzed, and as always, he both hoped and feared it was Thomas. He wanted to go over to Thomas' place, didn't want to go over, would not go unless he was invited. But it was a text message from Helen, and almost inevitably, it said 'So what do you think about those Sniggery Skeletons then?'

He called her straight away. 'Great minds, eh? I'm just

watching the news report now.'

'I knew it. Listen, that Dr. Rees is a colleague of mine - Theology and Archaeology are in the same building - and she's notoriously hopeless. She's only interested in getting on TV. And that's why she'll make professor long before me. So - how do you fancy doing your dissertation on local burial customs?'

'But I've already started on anchorites...'

'I don't mean really, I mean just pretend, so we can get in to see the skeletons. It's really annoying that you're not a policeman anymore, but I have my ways...'

Chapter Eight

In the foyer of the university's Forensic Archaeology department, Amber Rees bustled out to greet them, looking emphatically busy. She brought them into the laboratory, where the skeletons had been laid out; jigsaws of bones put back together on a series of brushed steel tables. There were two white-coated students examining and labelling one.

'Well, here we are, our new treasure trove!' said Dr Rees brightly. Darren and Helen tried to take in the room. Darren had spent plenty of time in forensic pathology labs, seen his fair share of unpleasant scenes of death, but he had never seen this many bodies in one place.

'Are these all from the woods?' he asked. 'How many are there?'

'Twenty.'

Darren felt himself a little triggered. That seemed to be the word people were using nowadays. He hated that word, which for him smacked of social media and snowflakes and people fussing about nothing. But the sight of a skeleton set in its body shape, surrounded by a rectangular frame, made him think of Matt in the ground, and he shook himself.

'So, you said that they date from the seventeenth century?'

'Ah, no. Well. Things have moved on since the news report. We have several mysteries here.'

She spoke as if she was presenting a BBC documentary, accentuating odd words, varying her pace and tone. Darren found it incredibly irritating.

'There are at least two that date back to the seventeenth century, those are the earliest. But the others are from all different time periods. Fascinatingly,' she said as she moved around the steel tables, addressing them as her audience, 'they all seem to be from slightly different time periods. Almost like a…'

'Like a chain?' said Helen.

'Yes, like a chain. We're still pinning them down using more advanced carbon dating techniques, but the most recent are twentieth century. In fact, this one here we estimate died in the Nineties.' She pointed to a set of bones that were lighter in colour than the rest, the skeleton almost completely intact.

'Wait. The 1990s? Thirty years ago? Do the police know this?' For a moment Darren had to remind himself that he was not on this case, and he felt a wave of frustration.

'Not yet, we're still doing our own investigation here.'

'Dr Rees, you need to call this in today. Promise me you will,' said Darren. She looked affronted at being spoken to like that by a student, so he softened. 'I used to be a policeman. I can guarantee the police need to know about this as soon as possible.'

'Yes, alright. I just didn't want the police to take away my beloved skeletons,' she said in a theatrically simpering voice.

Darren bristled with contempt, but he had Helen next to him, able as always to keep the tone bright. 'Are you able to tell how they died?' she asked.

'Now that's mystery number two. Some of these poor souls appear to have been bludgeoned to death. At least five are showing blunt force trauma on the skull, with no sign of healing, so that indicates perimortem trauma - that is, the injuries occurred at the time of death. The others - we can't tell yet how they died, but we are noticing a pattern.' She paused for effect before continuing, with a glint in her eye. 'Osteoporosis. Severe. Not normal osteoporosis, but a condition indicating that they were sedentary for a very very long time.' She put on gloves and held up one of the bones, addressing her students as well as Darren and Helen. 'Healthy bone looks like honeycomb under a microscope. Bones with osteoporosis look like honeycomb even without a microscope. And these bones have particularly large holes and spaces, a severe loss of density. It implies a prolonged lack of movement, and we see it most clearly in the knees and ankles. Disuse osteoporosis. And we don't see that on the poor bludgeoned fellows.'

'Are they all male then?'

'Ah no, sorry. I was just generalising. It's a mixture. Twelve female, eight male. It's quite clear from the shapes of the pelvises.'

'Any children?'

'No, all adults.'

'How can you tell? Is it the wisdom teeth?' asked Darren, noticing that not all the skulls still had teeth.

'No, it's the bone shafts that are more accurate determinants of age. The diaphysis and epiphysis are unfused in subadults, and these are all fused. In particular, the medial clavicle is fused on every skeleton, which indicates they were all mature adults, at least thirty years old.'

'What are your initial theories then?' asked Helen. 'A burial site? Could there possibly have been a graveyard there until the Nineties?'

'It's not possible,' said Darren. 'I used to play around there in the Nineties. There were no graves.'

'No, it's not a burial site. Because here's our third mystery.'

She gave a pause for effect, before saying 'These bones were only recently put there.'

Incredulous, Darren said 'How recently?'

'Very recently. This year. The mud was barely stuck to the bones.'

Darren and Helen looked at each other.

'Then someone knows about this.'

'Yes. Although a crime has not necessarily been committed.'

'You're clutching at straws there, Dr. Rees. You can't hold on to this any longer. This is a police matter. Promise me.'

She sighed. 'Yes, yes, I will. I just wanted to keep them with us for a few days, just so we could do our own research. I very much want to return these bodies' identities to them.'

'You've got more chance of doing that with the police involved. Do you have any other theories?'

'It's truly a mystery. And not all mysteries can be solved. I rather like that, don't you?'

As soon as they exited the building, Darren got out his phone. 'I need to call Colette.'

'Wait, Darren. Be careful not to get involved. You're not supposed to be here. And Rees said she would call the police so we have to let her do it now.'

'Yeah, you're right. And to be fair, she did give us a lot of information.'

They walked in silence for a while. Then Helen stopped and turned to him.

'Just say it. It's only me.'

'I think the two are connected. The wild woman and the bones. Nothing ever happens in Blundellsands, and then these two weird things happen together.'

'And. Say the next part.'

'A chain of bodies, who might have been imprisoned, and then a woman who looks like she has been indoors for a long time. Maybe since the Nineties.'

'And then the bones are discovered not long after the woman appears, and the two are connected.'

'Do you suspect that the woman dumped the bones somehow?'

'They have to be connected. There are no coincidences, right? And we can't just ignore the facts. There's a pattern.'

'That's a potentially unbroken chain of bodies, dating back to the seventeenth century. Ending when?'

'Well the last person appears to have died around, say thirty years ago?'

'Maybe the time that the Wild Woman went missing. It's

possible.'

He reminded himself that next time he saw Colette he would suggest she narrowed down her search to the 1990s. He wanted to call her now and tell her.

They walked in silence, lost in their own thoughts, drifting along the pavement next to each other. Strange images were forming in their minds, potential stories constructing themselves around two bare facts.

As if reading his mind again, Helen stopped and said 'I know you don't believe in coincidences, Darren, but I'm a firm believer in synchronicity.'

'What's the difference?'

'It's Carl Jung's theory to explain the paranormal. I know, I know, but hear me out. It's the principle of acausal connection. It was Jung's way of bringing the paranormal into the realms of intelligibility. Some people call it the intervention of grace, or meaningful coincidences; events that may not be linked by causality, but by some sort of meaning. And that meaning could be something outside of those events themselves; something that concerns your own life. Synchronistic events happen when people see a meaningful connection between external events and their own internal states. So most synchronistic events become explainable as reflections of what people are thinking and feeling.'

'It sounds like what you're saying is that this is all in our heads. That it's projection. Because we're going through things in our own lives.'

'No! That's not what I meant. Not quite. I'm just saying that synchronicity is there to make us more alert. To the possibilities of life. It propels us forward, gives us a surge of ephemeral courage, even if it doesn't mean anything.'

'I suppose things do feel more vivid again somehow. Like my inner world is connecting with the outside world again. Does that make sense?'

'Yes, exactly! And that's undoubtedly a good thing. There are infinite patterns in the universe, too many for us to cope with. We need a way to handle them. Synchronicity forces us to question our notions of what is scientific. There may be an answer, just not the one you were looking for. It fuels our intention. And it feels a bit magical. Synchronicity operates beyond simple cause and effect. Perhaps a policeman can't use it, but an academic certainly can.'

Chapter Nine

Darren's jogging and thinking had always been inextricably linked; he always had his best ideas while pounding the pavements. And his running almost invariably took him to Blundellsands, where the sand and dunes were soft on his knees, where the vast consoling sky allowed him space to breathe. Under that big sky, he felt comforted. What were problems when confronted with the inevitability of the tides, pulled by forces unseen from outer space? Darren always returned from the beach feeling cleansed, inspired, humbled. The wind roared past his ears and swept him clean.

On misty spring mornings like this, the city didn't feel quite real. The land and sea had been here before Liverpool, and would be here after it had gone. Everything had an unreal glaze, a sameness, almost sinister, as the haze removed visual clues for temporality. As his mind was filled with the puzzle of the skeletons, with thoughts of graveyards and cemeteries, he had a fleeting image of the air around him filled with restless souls, and the ground beneath his feet a bed of bones. The city built on the bodies of those who had gone before.

The water in this bay was not quite the sea, and not quite a river. It was deep grey and harsh. An estuary implied a sort of purgatory, a place in between, not one place or another. Time and space seemed to behave differently here. The dimensions and speed of a ship coming in would play tricks on the mind; one moment it would be a dot on the horizon, the next moment a giant monolith blocking the view, appearing almost within touching distance when in fact it was two miles out. This space seemed to have the power to temporarily erase fragments of memory, and Darren had plenty of memory fragments that he often wished to temporarily erase.

He usually kept to the coastline, his running rarely taking him into the streets, the wide avenues of Blundellsands itself. The houses here were oversized statements of plenty. There had always seemed to be something lonely, desolate about Blundellsands. The streets were always empty, the houses palimpsests on which family history after family history had been written and written over. Palatial yet forgotten, an air of ruin to the place even though its residents represented the triumphant, the economic elites. The sea was not the sea – it was just a giant river mouth, the real sea beginning miles out, marked by white waves and wind turbines. No shops, no restaurants, a non-place. Huge swathes of detached houses nestled in their grounds, mansion after mansion, each one different; their sheer size a provocation. Some dated back to the great merchant seamen; others were grand Edwardian houses, some converted into apartments. Then there were the modern follies, neo-Palladian columns, mock Tudor double-fronts, battlements and towers and stone lion gates.

And then there was the mile-long Sandy Lane, where earlier in his career Darren had used to work as a security officer at Thomas Kuper's house, during matches and away games, or around the time of a significant result. That was how Thomas had entered his life, and changed everything. So other feelings towards Blundellsands had crept in; no longer just boredom and bitterness, a world that was not his, but a world that held possibility. And now he was back visiting Sandy Lane regularly, no longer as Thomas' security guard but as his – his what? With their half-relationship still secret, Darren was still on the edge of things. It was still not quite his world.

He tried to see the area with fresh eyes, to get a different

Chapter Ten

During Thursday's lecture, Darren sensed that Helen had something to say to him, and guessed it probably wasn't about the very average paper he had handed in on the European Reformation. Her eyes were sparkling more than usual and she kept looking at him, or trying not to look at him, in a meaningful way. At the end of the lecture he approached the stage where she was hurriedly packing up.

'Shall we?'

She nodded with friendly urgency.

They left the building together and headed for the coffee shop automatically, and it gave Darren a warm feeling to think that this was now part of his new routine. Except that today was a little different. When they arrived, Mikko was already there at the window table which was becoming their regular place, and Darren noticed that not only did he not mind the change to the routine, he was glad to see him.

'So,' said Helen, when they were installed with coffees. She sat opposite them. 'We need to talk about secret societies.'

'Ok...' they both said at the same time.

Dismayed that it wasn't more obvious, Helen explained what she meant.

'A seemingly unbroken chain of bodies, going back to the seventeenth century. If Dr Rees' estimations are correct – and we have to assume that they are - I know I said she's a poor academic, but the carbon dating doesn't lie. If they're correct, that implies an organised process going back hundreds of years.

Whatever it means, whatever those skeletons were for or how they died – it was organised by a succession of people. They weren't individual cases – it's all part of the same case.'

'Ok...' They shifted in their chairs, listening intently.

'So, I've been looking into societies that have existed in Liverpool since the seventeenth century. And there aren't many. At one time Liverpool was full of them. The merchant seamen set them up when the city was on the rise, and for a century there was a flourishing café culture. But they declined in the late Victorian period, and the First World War just about finished them off. Apart from one. The Liverpool Natural Philosophy Society.'

She fished out some papers from her bag, print-outs from the society's website. 'It's rather secretive, and it's linked to the university but with an awkward relationship, as the society is not an accredited institution. I attended one of their public events once, a debate on evolution. I remember there was a speaker there who had some very unpleasant views on race. Someone who should never have been given a platform. They are what Mikko would describe as edgelords.'

'I've never used that term, dude, but sure, why not.'

'What are edgelords?' asked Darren.

'They like to court controversy, and they also revel in their mythical status.'

'So, this society is old?'

'Oh yes, that's exactly the point, it was founded in the early seventeenth century. They pride themselves on being older than the University. They own a lot of property, so they have the money to invite big name speakers; you know the types, the public intellectuals too risky for mainstream events. It's rather like a fraternity. Their figurehead is called James Absalom.'

'Oh, him,' said Darren. 'I think I've seen him on TV.'

Helen nodded. 'Yes, probably. He sometimes appears as a sort of talking head, usually taking the irreverent angle on some debate. And another thing. They have a religious connection. Natural philosophy was the name given to science back in the seventeenth century – science was still a form of religious study, albeit a dangerous one. Societies like this were set up to give scientists a safe space. Apparently, there is some mythical initiation ritual. I think they remodel themselves on the Knights Templar.'

'Aren't you interested to join?' asked Darren.

'Oh, I don't qualify because I follow a particular faith. They are all about syncretism, you know. Anyone who follows a particular faith or creed doctrine is automatically blackballed. But you would qualify though - you're a student.'

'Ok, I'll check it out. I like the sound of it actually – sounds very me. Atheist but interested in religion, eternal outsiders. Do they have any links to Blundellsands and Crosby?'

'Nothing I have seen. Except that it was founded by the wealthy merchant families, many of whom lived on the seafront down there. And that brings me to the only other society I've found dating back to that time… because it's based in Blundellsands.'

'Wait, what about churches though? There must be loads of old churches…'

'No, in fact. So many churches were destroyed in the Blitz. The oldest active church is early nineteenth century. So – anyway - this other society is called the Order of the Desert Fathers. They are an Italian order of monks, invited to Crosby during the recusancy period.'

'Wait, my English is failing me now,' said Mikko. 'Recusancy?'

'I don't know what it means either, Mikko,' consoled Darren.

'Sorry. Recusancy refers to Catholics who refused to convert to Protestantism during the Reformation. Crosby was a stronghold of recusancy in the early seventeenth century. There were priest holes everywhere. It's just a shame most of the buildings from that time were destroyed in the war, so there's little evidence of them now. Anyway, these monks were invited to minister the Catholic sacraments in secret to the Merchant family and their friends. They travelled from Italy in secret. And they never left. The monastery is still there on Belmont Avenue.'

'That's practically on the beach.'

'Exactly. It shouldn't be too hard for me to find a pretext for an appointment there. I am a theology lecturer after all.'

'And an ex-nun. Didn't you Sisters have social evenings with the monks?'

'No, never. Funnily enough, I didn't join a convent for the social events. Anyway-'

'You know,' said Mikko, apropos of nothing. 'Gerald Gardner was born in Blundellsands.'

Darren and Helen respectively said 'Who?' and 'Really?' at the same time.

'Gerald Gardner. He was basically the founder of the Wicca movement. Along with Aleister Crowley, he was the Father of modern occultism. Gardner was ordained into Aleister Crowley's Ordo Templi Orientis, whose core belief is "*Do what thou wilt shall be the Whole of the Law.*"

'If that's the rule in Blundellsands,' said Darren, 'then god help us. Money and a God complex is a bad combination.'

'He's actually a hero of mine. Total Depravity have a song called 'Cone Of Power'.

'Cone of Power?'

'You haven't heard of it? It's so cool. It was a ritual performed by Gardner and a bunch of witches in 1940, to ward off the Nazi invasion of Britain. They erected a Great Circle and formed a cone of power, magical energy sent to Berlin with the command of "you cannot cross the sea, you cannot come." It's all in our lyrics, man.'

Darren thought of the Starfish decoy defences along Crosby Beach. 'And conveniently for Gardner, the Nazis didn't invade.'

'I'm just saying,' Mikko winked.

As Helen and Mikko discussed some obscure occult text that interested them both for different reasons, Darren was quiet, thinking about how the most boring part of Liverpool was now transforming in his mind into something quite the opposite, something very strange indeed. He looked up Gerald Gardner on his phone. There was a sepia-toned photo of a wizened old man with a shock of white hair and a goatee beard, wearing black robes. He scrolled through the biography, and read '... *born to a wealthy merchant timber family... lifelong interest in weaponry... Rosicrucianism... Freemason... frequented nudist clubs...*' And sure enough, he was from Blundellsands.

'He was only born on the same street as that order of monks, just off the beach,' he said. 'They were almost next-door neighbours.'

Just that morning he had been wondering about what happened behind all those closed doors, and here was an answer. *Hidden forces.* And at the same time, it could easily be a collective fiction they were weaving between them. On his phone he googled 'secret societies in Liverpool' and smiled at the results. He held up his phone to show the others.

'Look - secret societies are in fashion, actually.'

Helen squinted at this phone. 'What am I looking at?'

'It's all bars. Liverpool has sprung up with private bars and clubs recently, it's the thing. Especially those speakeasies that have secret doors and passcodes.'

Darren remembered his clubbing days, when there was nothing more prestigious than getting into the VIP section. Now that he was with Thomas, he could get into any VIP section he wanted. Except that he couldn't, because they couldn't be open about their relationship.

Mikko rubbed his hands together. 'I have no problem with checking out a bunch of bars.'

But Darren felt irresponsible. Helen's research was fun, but this was all so frivolous.

'Of course, there are other explanations for those skeletons,' he said. 'What about re-interments? Cemeteries are periodically dug up. I can even think of one fairly recently in Bootle. There must be a list somewhere. Perhaps someone involved in a transfer of graves took a weird fancy to picking up some bodies. It's a bit of a coincidence about the successive time periods – but still – it's possible.'

'Well, dude, you are no fun at all,' said Mikko, slamming his hand on the table. 'I like the secret societies, let's go with that.'

Helen ignored him. 'Go on...'

'Sorry to burst the bubble. I just think there could be a more mundane explanation. There's also the possibility of a grave-robber, or a theft from a lab or museum…'

Darren was taken with the idea of a burial place being disturbed, perhaps a burial place that wasn't an official cemetery at all. He reminded himself to tell Colette to look into recent planning permissions.

Mikko said 'There's also the possibility that it's a super-secret society. Because there are two types of secret societies. Those that pride themselves on their hidden knowledge, gaining mythological power from it. Like this Natural Philosophy set-up. And then there are those that we don't even know about. Super-secret. Their power comes from the secret of their very existence. I think we're looking for one of those.'

'There might be something in that,' nodded Helen. 'It was in the early seventeenth century that Rosicrucianism first appeared in Europe, and they had all of these aberrant fringes and offshoots, secrets within secrets. If the group we're looking is an offshoot, it doesn't even have to be as old as the seventeenth century. For example, the Guardians of Truth – you know, Jared Case and Truth Fest - it's an offshoot of the Puritan movement. which has been around since the seventeenth century. Direct descendants, direct line. They have just modernised their methods.'

Darren remembered what Helen had told him about looking in the margins. The aberrant fringes. A society itself could be completely innocent, while at the same time a front for something very different.

'Ok, so a super-secret society. But if it's super-secret, how do we find it?'

'And if it's been going for centuries, why has the chain been broken now?'

'Maybe it hasn't. Maybe they already have their next victim.'

As they talked, Mikko had been elaborately preparing a cigarette, his tattooed, heavily ringed fingers expertly tipping, shaping and rolling tobacco into a paper, repeating the motions over and over as an unconscious ritual. He tapped the finished product on the table and indicated he was going outside to smoke.

Helen's and Darren's eyes had been so drawn to his hand movements that they kept on staring at the table, where he had left his phone. Throughout their conversation it had been repeatedly flashing into life as messages appeared, and a new one appeared now.

'Popular guy,' said Darren.

'Yes, I suppose,' said Helen, as they finally blinked their eyes away. They had both seen that the series of messages on Mikko's phone screen were from Jared Case.

Chapter Eleven

Darren signed up for a couple of forthcoming events run by the Liverpool Natural Philosophy Society. The topics couldn't have been more different; Islam, transgender rights, abortion, climate change; all with quirky headlines. The only factor linking them seemed to be their potential for controversy. No inflammatory subject was off-limits and the titles were creatively provocative: 'Is God The Ultimate Meme?', 'Whither Drag Queens', 'Abort This!' He saw an event scheduled for September that featured Jared Case, the creationist guy from the pub, and worryingly, Andrew Shepherd appeared to be signed up for an August debate on Heaven and Hell. Darren made a mental note to warn Shepherd, next time he bumped into him, not to take part in that event under any circumstances. Apart from anything else, it would break the terms of his probation if he talked in public about his case.

Darren sent an email to the contact address on the Society's website, introducing himself as a mature student interested in joining. He titled the email 'Membership Enquiry.' Relishing his new freedom to try out different personas, he wrote 'Hi! I'm Darren Swift, a theology student at Liverpool University. I'd love to attend the following upcoming events...'

He wondered if that was the first time he had ever used an exclamation mark in an email. To Darren's surprise, while he was still re-reading the email he had just crafted and sent, marvelling at the uncharacteristic enthusiasm he had managed to convey, he received a reply. From a 'Nicole', secretary to

James Absalom, with a proposed appointment at eleven o'clock on Monday.

And so, on Monday morning he found himself on Upper Duke Street, in the historic merchants' quarter of the city, looking at a classy gold plaque which announced that the grand town house, Horrox House, in front of him was the Liverpool Natural Philosophy Society. It also proclaimed that it was 'Members Only, or by appointment.'

Upper Duke Street was an assortment of nightclubs, derelict warehouses and luxury apartments; only some of the original grand Georgian terraced facades remained, and behind those were even fewer of the original structures. Darren had done as much research as he could on the society, which was in the curious position of being prominent in the media, yet secretive and with a cultivated status of being 'misunderstood.' It had been founded in 1638 by Jeremiah Horrox, one of Liverpool's eclectic mix of famous sons that Darren hadn't known about, and Horrox's friend William Crabtree. Jeremiah Horrox was the astronomical prodigy who, along with Crabtree, was the first to predict and view the Transit Of Venus in 1639. Born to a Puritan family in Toxteth, Horrox ended up at Cambridge University, but his great observation was made from his own home-made observatory near Liverpool. It was a more controversial discovery than might first appear, since it corroborated Copernicus' revolutionary theory that the planets orbited the sun. Blasphemous work in its time, and the notoriety gained by Horrox and Crabtree brought them to the attention of local trader William Merchant, who financed Horrox's observatory and championed the ideal of scientific freedom. In fact, his idea predated the Royal Society by several decades. Natural Philosophy at that time meant science. It was not called by its name; it was a blend, and Horrox himself was a poet as well as an astronomer. Horrox's death at the age of twenty-two, followed by the Civil War, left the society languishing for a while, but William Merchant distinguished himself in the war and went on to become one of the first great shipping merchants of Liverpool's golden age. Many other societies sprang up after this, as Liverpool's café society developed, but with its property and endowment, this was the society that survived.

The door buzzed open and Darren found himself in a grand hallway, double the width of the frontage of the house, with portraits on the walls and a sweeping dark oak staircase. To the left of the staircase on the ground floor was a work site, boarded up for some renovation project, so with nowhere else to go, Darren mounted the staircase. At the top was a beautiful stained-glass window depicting Horrox, he presumed, in wig and gown, with his telescope, observing Venus. He turned the corner and entered a spacious reception area, all plush red carpets, with an unmanned reception desk and a small bar area. To the right of the desk was a plexiglass wall behind which was a library with floor-to-ceiling books, many of them leather-bound series. Two people were inside the library studying at desks, but Darren was unable to get a good look at them, because a door in the oak-panelling to the left of him opened, and James Absalom appeared.

'Hello, Darren Swift? Come in.'

Darren recognised him instantly from various late-night television appearances. He was regularly brought in as a talking-head on discussion panels, almost invariably taking the controversial side. His internet tv show, The Heretics, had begun as a podcast, and had grown into a fortnightly show filmed in the city's Saturn Theatre, with almost a million viewers and a paying live audience. The camera loved him with his impossibly classic good looks and acerbic eloquence. His accent had a soft Liverpool lilt, far more sophisticated, Darren thought, than his own harsh sing-song voice. It was almost impossible to win an argument against this man, and many had fallen live on television trying. He over-enunciated; inserting complex words into long, effusive sentences that each had the character of a revelation.

Ordinarily he would be the type of person Darren hated, but he was strangely drawn, not just to the man's charisma, but to the whole ethos of the place. It all seemed to make sense somehow. It wasn't afraid to open cans of worms, to explore dark corners. It was open to possibilities, however strange.

James Absalom led him into his office, which had a huge bay window overlooking Duke Street and decorated with stained glass panels. It was how Darren imagined a gentleman's club to be. A real one. In fact, it was almost a caricature of a gentleman's club – not a trope had been missed. There was even a smell of leather and cigars. The only clue as to its possible inauthenticity was Absalom's attire. He was wearing trousers that looked too tight, the sort of trousers Darren would never wear, slightly too short, and infuriatingly, he didn't wear socks with his pointed black brogues. His t-shirt was also tight-fitting and proclaimed the logo of some Japanese computer game.

There was a huge oak desk, replete with red leather inlay and green reading lamps, but James motioned to two burgundy leather armchairs in the window.

'What can I get you – coffee? tea? Early gin and tonic?'

'Coffee, please, if you're having one…'

'No caffeine for me, but we have an excellent coffee machine in the bar, let me ask Nicole,' and he texted something into his phone.

'I feel like I'm in a period drama' Darren said, admiring his surroundings as he sank into his chair. There couldn't be many of these buildings left in Liverpool, not intact like this. The richly-hued carpet, soft-lighting from fringed shades, antique furniture and two walls loaded with bookshelves right up to the stucco ceiling; it all conveyed a sense of timelessness and a reverence for the past.

'Is that a real Turner?' Darren motioned to a gilded frame containing an ethereal scene of ships on a misty Mersey, impressed at himself that he might have recognised a painter.

'It is, yes. Always been here. And next to it,' Absalom said with gravitas, 'is the portrait of our founder, Jeremiah Horrox. Romanticised, of course. We don't know if he actually looked like that. I like to think that he did. And he certainly wrote the poem.'

He motioned to Darren to get up, follow him over to admire the painting. It was the same image as the stained glass, which had obviously been modelled on the painting.

Horrox wore scholarly black robes, with a white ruffle and the black brimmed hat of the time. His telescope was set up at the window and he had one hand raised to point at the sky, the other raised in explanation to the painter, his audience. Confident yet earnest, beholding a miracle, explaining a miracle. His posture reminded Darren of James Absalom, and Darren wondered if Absalom modelled his mannerisms on his predecessor.

Next to the painting of Horrox was a plaque engraved with verse:
Thy return posterity shall witness
Years must roll away,
But then at length the splendid sight
Again shall greet our distant children's eyes
The clouds which once obscured our mental sight
Are gone forever; great Copernicus... lays open to our view
The arduous secrets of wide Heaven's domain.
Turn hither then your grateful steps, for here
Are wondrous mysteries that you may learn,
Open to all whom... The love of truth impels.

They read it in silence together, unconsciously mimicking each other's folded arms.

'It's beautiful, isn't it?' said Absalom, leading him back to the armchairs.

'It sounds like he's talking about the Second Coming.'

'Yes. It's very clever. Because of course he's actually talking about the transit of Venus, and even more, about Copernican heliocentrism. The planets going round the sun. That was the height of blasphemy in its time, but he was able to conflate it with language that could also be attributed to God.'

'I suppose it would be dangerous for scientists back then to suggest that God didn't exist.'

'It's dangerous now! More so than ever in today's sensitive climate. Even Stephen Hawking didn't deny the possibility of God. Horrox studied unseen forces. He used that exact phrase. Unseen forces – and there lies the Venn diagram between science and religion. We are all searching for things hidden since the foundation of the world.'

Darren loved that description. He loved the idea of unseen forces. It resonated with everything that had happened over the past two years. In fact, so far, he liked everything this man said.

They moved along the wall to the next oil painting.

'Next to that is his benefactor, of course, William Merchant, who happens to be an ancestor of mine. Sort of. So, in a sense, you are. In a period drama, I mean. If they ever make a series about eighteenth century merchant seamen, they will come knocking. Actually, my immediate predecessor here used to dress in almost period costume; cravats, breeches, tail coats, that sort of thing. It's not for nothing that we have been accused of attention-seeking.'

Absalom and his laptop were the only clues to modernity in this room. There was a plethora of memorabilia from Liverpool's great age of sea merchants, including a large golden ship's bell. The shipping age was tainted by slavery, but this organisation had been set up before slavery had begun, and noted members were abolitionists. There was little to criticise, in fact; it was infuriatingly clean.

'So, what can I do for you?' Absalom asked as they sat back in leather armchairs. Nicole glided in with their drinks and then out again silently. From the effortless way they interacted, or didn't interact, plus their matching good looks, Darren assumed that Nicole and James must be married.

'I was just interested in maybe joining the society. To be honest, I didn't think I'd be meeting you in person today. I guess I'm in luck.'

'I happened to have a window this morning. And the luck is all mine. So... what's your interest?'

'Right. I'm studying theology, a Masters at Liverpool Uni, and a lot of your past publications and lectures have been relevant to my course, so I thought...'

'Ah, just to stop you there. While for historical reasons we take a special interest in the Christian intellectual tradition, we don't allow members who subscribe to a particular faith. There's a long history of esotericism here.'

'Well that's why I'm here, actually. I'm studying esoteric Christianity this term, in fact, as part of the course. But I'm not religious at all, no worries. I just found some of the ideas on your website appealing.' And it was true, he did. A lot of it made sense, particularly after the events of the past two years.

'You said you had questions. Fire away.'

Darren decided to start with something bland and practical, reminding himself that this was not an interrogation. If anything, he was the one being tested.

'The membership fee of five hundred pounds. What's it used for? I don't mind, it's just that my budget is tight, you know.'

Absalom opened his hands apologetically. 'The short answer is that it's to put people off, to be quite honest with you. People are welcome to attend the events, to watch on the internet. But we don't want thousands of members, and we certainly don't want people joining in order to try and cause trouble. It's supposed to be one of these safe spaces that everyone talks about nowadays. But a space for radical viewpoints.'

'The other thing is the initiation rite that I've heard about. I'm not sure I fancy it. Does it put people off? I mean, can you opt out?'

James had already started to laugh knowingly as Darren spoke, nodding his head as if unsurprised at the question. He leaned back in his chair and folded his arms, looking up to the ceiling in light-hearted irritation.

'I know which newspaper you've read. There's a particular journalist who took umbrage with the way I defeated him in a TV debate, and he's been after me ever since. But this ritual idea, it's mainly urban myth. And I can't stand all those Oxbridge style hustings and humiliations. There is a welcome ceremony, it's true, a simple ritual that's been done for hundreds of years, but it's nothing like those ridiculous Freemason-style things. Just a promise to abide by our rules. Like a wedding, a degree ceremony, a sports award, a funeral… life is full of rituals, there's nothing sinister about it. The main membership requirement is to attend at least three of our events before you can join. Then you wait to be invited.'

'By you?'

'By me. That keeps the tabloid journalists out.'

'But any journalist can attend one of your public events though…'

'Yes, but only membership confers access to our private events, our library, our contacts list, our bar...'

'Why *are* you so secretive? Is it just marketing?'

Absalom smiled a wry smile. 'It is a brand, for sure. The urban myths that surround us are quite fun, so we don't always debunk them. There were rumours that one of my predecessors was a friend of Hitler, there were whispers about Satanic abuse back in the Victorian days, you name it. It's all fun and games.

'But we are secretive for the same reasons that we *were*

secretive. It's more than a tradition, it's a necessity. Remember that in Jeremiah Horrox's time, science and religion were one, and dissenting ideas were dangerous. So, this was a safe space then. And we have rather come full circle, don't you think?'

'In what way?'

'This society was founded because people were afraid of truth. Religion was orthodoxy, and anything that questioned the prevailing orthodoxy was quashed. Then came the age of science, when science trumped religion and superstition, when truth mattered most. There was a time when this society was perhaps surplus to requirements. And now we are in the age of – what? Post-truth, perhaps. The age of stupidity, certainly. Truth-telling, or even questioning the norm, these have become dangerous activities. We need that protection again, and our work is more important than ever. I presume you've heard of cancel culture? It purports to protect free speech, but in reality, it's the opposite.

'So, there you go. We've been called edgelords, clickbaiters, intellectual bottom feeders. But we have only ever been truth-seekers. And everyone is afraid of the truth. Just the same as when we were founded.'

'What are you afraid of?' asked Darren.

'Infiltration. There are dangers. Have you seen what happens outside abortion clinics? What happens when universities invite right-leaning speakers? We may not risk being burned at the stake, but being scapegoats? We are sceptics not in the cynical sense, but in the scientific sense. And I think you are too. You seem sceptical, Darren, and I like that. I imagine that's why you are studying theology?'

Darren almost mentioned his childhood, but then held back, and offered only 'I have a lot of questions, I suppose.' He felt utterly unjudged by this man, as if he could tell him anything.

'You look old for a student, if you don't mind me saying.'

'I'm a mature student. I was in the police force before.

Detective Inspector.' Darren winced at himself for wanting to impress Absalom. He hadn't even planned to reveal he was a policeman.

'A truth-seeker indeed,' said Absalom, without batting an eyelid. 'So, you're old for a student, but young to reach the rank of detective - how old are you? Again, if you don't mind me asking?'

'Thirty-three. It's the Jesus year, apparently. Someone told me the other day. I noticed you have quite a few religious speakers, some of whom I would have called crazy. For want of a better word.'

'Yes, and we don't invite them to make fun of them. We don't treat creationists and flat-earthers and crazy conspiracy theorists any more like crazy people than we do astrophysicists and radical feminists. Because there's nothing crazier than human life. Do you want to be the one who dismisses as ridiculous something that later turns out to be crucial to humanity's future? Let's take a moment, examine the evidence, then we can throw it out if appropriate. We simply follow the Principle of Laplace: "the weight of the evidence should be proportioned to the strangeness of the facts."'

Darren thought of his recent cases, the strangeness of the facts – he had buried himself in evidence. And yet there were still so many things that could not be explained.

'Although,' continued Absalom, 'there's no denying the benefits of a bit of controversy. Social media is a part of what we do - how could it not be?'

Darren hated social media, and wondered how Absalom could lower himself to interacting with all those people online, those trolls and keyboard warriors. But other than that, he couldn't disagree with a single thing this man had said. In fact, he felt they saw eye to eye on a lot.

'How many new members do you get every year?' asked Darren, more for something to keep to conversation going than out of genuine interest.

'You ask a lot of questions, Darren.'

'Sorry. Sometimes I forget I'm not a policeman anymore.'

And it was true. He had been enjoying the freedom from protocol and constraint that his new civilian role gave him. But it was never going to work if his go-to method of making conversation was interrogation. He got up to leave, and Absalom showed him back into the lobby.

'The library out there is amazing.' He tried to take it in as they walked past. 'Do members have access?'

'Yes. To most of it, anyway. We have a lot of texts that are really not found anywhere else. The British Library would love to get their hands on them.' They reached the top of the oak staircase. 'Sorry about the building works.' Absalom motioned down to the temporary plywood that blocked part of the hallway. 'We're doing some renovations. Next time you come, the hall should be restored to its former glory. Well, Darren, I look forward to seeing you at an event soon. Perhaps…'

They shook hands, and Absalom touched his arm, lingering a moment longer than would have been expected and looking him directly in the eyes.

Darren emerged into the sunlight and traffic feeling energised, his mind opened to new possibilities. That man made him feel intelligent. The presumptuous overuse of his first name was a classic technique, he knew, but it worked on him anyway. Darren, more often than not, made a bad impression on people, with his awkward, abrupt manner. It made a change to be so liked, so understood.

Chapter Twelve

It wasn't difficult for Helen to manufacture a reason to visit the Order of the Desert Fathers. She was a theology lecturer looking for local guest speakers, and there was an unusual Catholic sect nestled right within the community. The connection was so obvious it could conceivably have happened already, and Helen was in the process of convincing herself that she did want Father Angelo Zotti to give a talk to her History of Christianity class. Because if that wasn't the case, then what on earth was she doing? Investigating the monks' connection to some vague notion of kidnapping and murder going back centuries? It was too ridiculous to contemplate.

Whatever the case, this was a very interesting organisation. The Order of the Desert Fathers was founded in the 1300s in Italy. It was a missionary order with records of visits to the north of England dating back to the Middle Ages. During the wars of religion, this part of Liverpool - Crosby and its surroundings - had been a hotbed of recusancy, and the ruling Lunt family had invited the Order of the Desert Fathers to minister secret Catholic services to recusant worshippers. This was dangerous work – the few surviving houses in the area from that period had evidence of priest holes. Discovery would result in torture and death for both worshipper and minister, and often did.

The Order was richly rewarded for their daring and loyalty, and invited to set up a permanent chapter in the area. The location of their original dwelling had passed into obscurity, but around the 1800s they had moved to Belmont House in Blundellsands, and had never left.

The monks' set-up appeared far more modern than Helen's old order, the Sisters Of Grace; they had a website filled with glossy images, almost like a hotel brochure, advertising the House as a conference centre or retreat, and on the welcome page there was a large photo of the prior, Father Angelo Zotti. He was now waiting for Helen on the steps of Belmont House as she pulled into the driveway. The building was a typical merchants' mansion, if there was such a thing, since every house in this area was completely unique. All large bay windows and double-fronts, its red-brick facades had been added to over the years with various extensions, plus a brand-new single-storey wing. It was a mish-mash of faded largesse and modern functionality. The plot was large and Helen had seen from the website that the back garden was whimsical, with little Christian follies here and there – a cupola, a Virgin's shrine, a little footbridge over a pond.

It couldn't have been built any earlier than the 1800s when the monks moved in. Helen resolved to find out who had built and financed it, because that piece of information was missing from the extensive history on the website, as well as the location of the monks' original dwelling.

Father Zotti was slight, middle-aged, and had an intense aquiline face. Helen was relieved that his hair was close-shaved, rather than that tonsure which she had always found to be a look somehow far more undignified than the nun's habit. *And that is yet another reason why I should never have been a nun*, thought Helen. *You're not supposed to find monks attractive or otherwise.* Even from this distance, Father Zotti exuded the natural calm, kindness and authority typical to the clergy, and looked almost papal in his cream-coloured robes. He also looked typically scouse with his wiry proportions, close-cropped hair, and a particularly wry expression on his face, she noticed, as she got out of the car and prepared her smile.

'Dr Hope, I recognise that car! The Sisters Of Grace, surely!' He walked around it, admiring, after shaking her hand. 'There can't be many others like that around... and there, I can see the little silver cross on the bumper.'

Helen still had the ancient green Volkswagen Beetle that had belonged to the Sisters Of Grace; she and Sister Mary had been the only members of the Order with driving licences, and so Deaconess Margaret had given it to Helen as a parting gift. She couldn't help feeling guilty at taking it, even though, as Mikko reminded her, she had more than earned it after donating her university salary to the convent for ten years. And with Sister Mary spending the rest of her days in prison, it was unlikely any of the elderly sisters were going to learn to drive. At the thought of the convent she felt guilty again, because she realised that she could be unwelcome here. A lapsed nun? Having broken the vows for which that these men had given their lives? And now back in the house of God. She felt uneasy in a new way, but if the abbot disapproved, he didn't show it.

'Now I'm putting a face to a name – you're Sister Helen! Sorry, Dr. Helen now, of course.' His accent was a gentle combination of Italian and Liverpudlian. Helen adored the combination accents of immigrants to the city, so common nowadays. The local accent was incredibly infectious and quickly took over.

'Deaconess Margaret often talked about you. She and I go back a long way. I used to enjoy our monthly glasses of wine. Sadly, they have tailed off since... well, since the unfortunate events. Do send her my regards when you next see her.'

'I will, of course.' Helen resolved to telephone the Deaconess soon, another duty in which she had lapsed. She noted that she hadn't even set foot in the monastery building yet, and she was already feeling weighed down by multiple guilts.

Father Angelo ushered her through the large entrance hall into a drawing room. The smell was immediately familiar; the smell of the passing of time, clean yet musty, old slightly damp books, threadbare furniture, tea and cake. It smelled like the convent, and memories flooded back. Father Angelo was pouring tea and telling her an anecdote about Deaconess Margaret. Helen smiled at the thought of the two of them having their secret wine-drinking sessions together; Margaret had never said a word about it, and Helen had barely heard of this place in the ten years she had spent at the Sisters of Grace, even though there couldn't have been many religious orders in the area. They could have been having monks-and-nuns socials all along, she thought, and almost snorted out loud with laughter, giddy with nerves at the situation.

Tea poured, Father Angelo sat down and clasped his hands, and there was silence for a moment. Helen had no doubt that his performed serenity was powerful. She almost felt sleepy, her nerve endings softened and relaxed. She looked at her surroundings. They were in the equivalent of the convent's 'day room', although this place was a better-funded version. The armchairs and sofas were plush and matching instead of threadbare and assorted; the shelves stocked with modern volumes as well as tattered old books; and at one end stood a huge work table of modern lacquered wood, laid out with the day's newspapers and a selection of ecumenical publications. To her right, patio doors led out onto the side-garden. There was a monk out there, an anorak on top of his robes, bent over to weed a flower bed. Helen suddenly had a vision of the wild woman, in the ragged skirts she imagined her wearing, bent double as she foraged for shellfish on the beach.

The ticking of an antique grandfather clock in the corner emphasised the silence. It was almost an aggressive sound, an affront. A reminder of the relentless passing of time. As if reading her mind, Father Angelo said, 'I imagine this environment is bringing up some memories for you?'

'Yes, I suppose. I…'

She hoped he would finish her sentence for her, with something to make her feel better, but he left it hanging for a while, like a counsellor would, kindly, before finally he helped her out. 'It's alright. God decided on a different path for you. Anyway,' he livened up his tone, 'how can I help you?'

'I was wondering if we could explore opportunities for collaboration with the university. We have guest speakers and it would be wonderful to have someone local.'

'We'd be delighted. As you will have seen from the website, we are an open community here, very involved with the outside world. I'm surprised we haven't been asked before, actually. Perhaps it's the missionary aspect that has put you academics off. That word, missionary, does make people uncomfortable. Truthfully it makes me uncomfortable too, it has the wrong connotations nowadays. It implies compulsion, and that's not at all what we are about.'

'Yes, we'd have to play down that part. I was thinking about local history, actually. I'm teaching the History of Christianity course this year - this area was such a stronghold of recusancy, and your connection with that is fascinating. I read that the Order has been active around here since the seventeenth century?'

'Indeed, we have. We were invited here by the Lunt family and, what can I say? We liked the place, so we never left.'

'But this house only dates back to the 1800s. Where were you before?'

There was a pause. He was looking at her with an entirely neutral expression on his face, and Helen wondered if her question had come out rather oddly. Why would she care about where they were before?

'Do you know, I'm not entirely sure,' he said. 'The abbot really should know, shouldn't he? You have inspired me to go back into our records.'

Out of the corner of her eye Helen sensed another figure in the garden. A man in brown robes, with an incongruous sports hoodie over the top, was walking alone, ponderously. He was holding a closed Bible and looking up the sky, a slightly strained expression, as if he was trying to remember or memorise something.

'Perhaps,' she said, still looking outside, 'it would be nice to have someone young – it's such an unusual choice for young people, and I think our students would be fascinated.'

'You have spotted our latest initiate, Owen. It's not as unusual as you think, in fact. We always have an initiate on the go, as it were. We never leave the line unbroken. He will take his vows in a few weeks, and as you can see he's studying hard.'

'Shall we go and ask him?' said Helen.

'Ask him?'

'If he'd like to speak to our students?'

Father Angelo smiled. 'I'm afraid you won't get anything out of him. He's taken a vow of silence this week. We all do, regularly.'

Helen's heart sank. The novice looked towards the house and, for a moment, their eyes met; or perhaps he was looking at the abbot; perhaps he couldn't see them at all. He appeared to be in his late twenties, and it was hard to tell from this distance but she thought she could see tattoos on his neck. She tried to read his facial expression, but couldn't.

'Do you mind me asking what his story is?' She turned to the abbot. 'I'm just… it's rare to see a young novice nowadays and, since I was one myself…'

'No, I don't mind at all. And like I said, it's not as unusual as you might think. Owen came to us via a half-way house where we do outreach work. He was struggling to rejoin society after prison – not a qualification to his name and no family to speak of either.'

'What had he done?'

'Drug-related offences. And worse. Violent crimes. He carried a heavy burden of guilt; sinning had become a way of life for him, and we are helping to lift that burden.'

Catherine Fearns

Helen felt – *what do I feel?* she asked herself. *Concerned?* No, what she felt was an ominous foreboding, a desperate urge to save this boy. *Am I projecting?* She asked herself, and knew that she was. But she was sure there was something in his eyes, some uncertainty. And nobody should make that sort of commitment without certainty.

'He has found peace with us here,' said the abbot, kindly but firmly. The young man was now smiling and laughing with the gardening monk, and Helen shook herself. *Do I feel uncomfortable here because of me, or because of something else?* Guilt as a way of life. How familiar that sounded.

She looked at the shelves of books which took up the whole back wall of the room. From her position a few metres away she could make out sections on history, different religions, lives of the saints, a mixture of well-thumbed paperbacks and grand leather-bound volume collections.

'You have an impressive library here,' she noted.

'Ah, yes, that's just the half of it. We also have a library next to the chapel, with our more sacred texts.'

'May I look at your catalogue? I'd be fascinated to see what you have. I'm always looking to update our library at the university.'

He smiled that unbreachable smile again. 'I'm afraid that's not possible. We pride ourselves on our particular teachings, only available to the initiated, and so our sacred library is private.'

Foiled, Helen had nothing else, and decided to end the meeting, and bring this monk out of his environment onto her territory at the university. She looked out again to the garden, beyond which was the beach, only a few hundred metres from the area where the wild woman was found. The monks' garden was busy and characterful, in the English gothic revival style designed to evoke a pastoral idyll. She scanned the garden's features; rolling lawns, beds of herbs, the histrionic pose of the Virgin Mary statue, a well-covered by a stone cupola, a wooden shed. What am I looking for? She wondered. A hiding place? A clue? She suddenly felt very childish.

Chapter Thirteen

Darren held his head in his hands. 'How could I have been so fucking stupid?'

Across the table in the Crown & Anchor, Mikko and Helen were doubled over with laughter, and next to him even the usually circumspect Thomas was laughing.

'Stop, it hurts to laugh this much.' At the head of the table Colette put one hand on Darren's arm to comfort him, the other one clutched at her side. Finally, Darren raised his red face and allowed himself to laugh too.

'What's the joke then?' the barmaid asked as she came over to collect glasses.

Colette composed herself. 'Darren went to a sex club.' And then she crumpled again. 'Of all the people I can't imagine in a…'

'Actually, I'm starting to get offended now. Why is it so ridiculous that I would go to a..?'

'Go on, you can say it, Darren.'

Darren's conversation with Mikko and Helen about Gerald Gardner, the occultist who had turned out to be born in Blundellsands, had made him think of something. Gardner. The Gardner Club. It rang a bell, and it was something local, but he didn't know why. Nothing came up on the internet, nothing at all, but he was sure he had heard of something called The Gardner Club. It mildly bothered him for a couple of days, until he was in the supermarket queue and glanced at the community noticeboard. He had always made a point of looking at this noticeboard; it was part of his job as a policeman to know what was going on in the community. And there it was – a small ad, printed on cheap fluorescent pink paper and pinned there so long ago it was dog-eared and a little faded. It said *The Gardner Club*, in a plain font, and underneath: '*Are You Curious?*' Then there was a phone number. That was it! That was the sign he had seen pasted surreptitiously on lampposts and walls around Crosby and Waterloo, in passing, over the course of years, countless times, without giving them a second thought. They had just been part of the environment, one of the miniature mysteries you don't bother to question.

Back at home, he had looked up the phone number, and although it was ex-directory, it had a local dialling code. He called, and it was answered by a female with a sing-song Liverpool accent, in the old-fashioned way of answering the phone: '4557?'

'I'm calling about The Gardner Club?'

'Oh, right love, sorry. Is it your first time?'

'Er, yeah.'

'Lovely. So, we meet on the second Thursday of every month, and we give out the address to newcomers on the night. The only question we ask is: Are You Curious?'

'Erm. Yes.'

'Ok brilliant. So, you'll receive a text to this number with the payment details – it's one hundred pounds to join. And if we receive the payment, then you'll receive another text on the night, giving you the address, and the rules. No phones, no weapons, and there will be security.'

'Just one question: can I bring someone?'

'Yes, you can love. But that will be two hundred pounds. As I say, that does give you both memberships.'

Darren put the phone down feeling as if he had just made a hairdressing appointment. But this had to be something occult. Wasn't 'Are You Curious?' the question that was whispered to Freemasons? Two hundred pounds… that was a lot. But this was an avenue that had to be explored; he couldn't ignore the possibility that the name Gardner could be significant. A secret society here in Crosby - that was exactly what they were looking for. Not wanting to put Thomas at risk – and indeed, was there anywhere he could safely bring Thomas, he was beginning to think with no small amount of bitterness - not wanting to mention to Colette that he was conducting his own parallel investigation, and not really having any other close friends, Darren had called and asked Mikko to come with him.

'Do I want to check out a secret occult society? Does the pope shit in the woods?'

On Thursday evening, Darren received a single text, listing an address on the fringe of Blundellsands, near the railway station. It was one of those huge four-storey terraces with windowed basements that had formerly been servants' quarters, and were now mostly apartments. The promised 'rules' had not been sent however, so he and Mikko arrived at the address knowing nothing about what was going to happen. They rang the doorbell and waited, Mikko shuffling back and forth on his feet, hands in his pockets, and noticing the domestic paraphernalia that littered the front porch and front garden. An old pram, potted plants, discarded gardening gloves, a faded plastic tractor for toddlers. 'It's a pretty disappointing entrance to the headquarters of a satanic cult. Are you nervous?'

'I don't know. I don't even know what this is. Thanks for coming.'

'Any time, man.'

They heard footsteps and saw a shadow behind the door. The moment it opened Darren knew the mistake he had made. The corridor was red-lit, the music was thudding ambient bass noise, and there were shadowy figures moving in the back – that was all satanic enough - but the woman who opened the door, and he recognised her voice as the one who he had spoken to on the phone, was wearing tacky and ill-fitting red lace lingerie. Pink flesh bulged out here and there. She looked momentarily surprised.

'Oh, we usually get straight couples. But that's fine,' she said brightly, beckoning them through. 'Come in, come in. I forgot to send you the rules, if you wouldn't mind having a look at this and signing, before you get comfortable, you know. It's all common sense, nothing controversial. No need to put your real name, obviously.' She handed Darren a clipboard and trotted towards the kitchen in her kitten heels. 'Come on, it's alright. Get yourselves a drink, you've paid for them!' Darren scanned the clipboard, seeing phrases like *'the dungeon master is there to ensure your safety… observe designated safe words… don't touch anyone without permission… above all, HAVE FUN!!'*

Darren and Mikko shuffled along the corridor after her, glancing furtively into rooms to their left in which fleshy masses were moving, thrusting, and to their right, which appeared empty of people but there was an ominous-looking structure with straps and harnesses. The sideboard was lined with various implements and instruments, reminiscent of a buffet, which included a supply of baby wipes.

Following Darren, Mikko leaned up to whisper in his ear. 'Dude, I'm a pretty open-minded guy, but this is not my thing. Are you sure this is the place?'

'I'm really sorry. What shall we do?'

'Fucking leave, obviously.'

'What I don't understand,' said Colette through tears, 'is why you went inside?'

'I don't know, it just felt rude not to, you know what I mean?'

'It is so Darren Swift to go to a swingers' party out of politeness,' said Thomas.

'He even put his name down on the clipboard,' laughed Mikko.

'What name did you put?' asked Colette.

'DCI McGregor, obviously.'

'Well,' said Helen. 'You were at a sex club and I was at choir practice. That just about sums up our relationship, Mikko.'

When the notice said 'Are You Curious?' did it not even cross your mind that it might be a sex club, Darren?'

'I thought 'Are You Curious' was a Masonic thing. Isn't that what they ask you to find out if you're a Mason?'

'Ask DCI McGregor, I think he's one,' said Colette, downing her wine.

'He never is.'

'He is. I think so.'

They were laughing, but Darren was embarrassed at himself. How could he have made such a stupid call? Was he losing his touch?

'Do you think we're just bored? Do you think we are just inventing this story about the skeletons?'

'There has to be a simpler explanation. Occam's Razor, right?' said Colette. 'And may I remind you it's not your case to investigate, it's mine.'

'I'm not sure Occam's Razor applies in this case,' said Helen. 'Whoever put those bones there in the woods, and someone did, recently, *that* person has a complicated story to tell.'

'The simplest explanation is graves being reinterred due to change of land use.'

'You can fill your boots with that Darren, but I've been told to prioritise finding where this Wild Woman has been, and then identifying the most recent skeleton from the 90s. Now the skeletons are in the news, every man and his dog is getting in on the conspiracy theories, so Canning Place have told us to wrap it up quickly.'

'Identifying the most recent body would probably give us our answer actually.'

'When you think about someone just disappearing... it would have to be someone that nobody would look for,' said Colette. 'Not too hard, anyway. If I disappeared, there'd be a hundred odd people looking for me within hours.'

'Lucky you. I don't think anybody would miss me,' said Darren, kneeing Thomas.

'I would,' said Colette. 'Who would I have my Wednesday night pint with then?'

'DCI McGregor.'

'God. Darren, promise me you won't ever disappear.'

But Darren thought he probably could disappear, quite easily. If he went off to Madrid with Thomas, he'd be a ghost figure there, as the secret gay partner of a footballer. And who would miss him here? Really miss him? His parents lived three miles away, yet he hadn't spoken to them in years. Darren thought about ignominy. He could almost hear Absalom's voice talking about cancel culture, about how the greatest fear of the modern world was not to be noticed.

They were all playing the game.

Helen said 'My students would probably wonder why I hadn't turned up to lectures for a couple of weeks, but then I think that would be it. My mother certainly wouldn't look for me. And the nuns have rather disowned me. So, I don't think anyone would be too bothered really.'

'Er, hi,' said Mikko.

'Oh, apart from you of course.'

But Helen was thinking about Mikko and this dreadful Christian festival she had agreed to attend. She wondered what would happen if she didn't go, if they went their separate ways now, him back to Norway and her to Liverpool, and never contacted each other again. Would it be as if their relationship had never happened? Perhaps everything would go on as before and it would be like a strange dream.

'What a bunch of lost souls we are.'

'Speak for yourselves,' said Colette, checking her vibrating phone. 'DCI McGregor wants to release the Wild Woman's photo to the press - he's under pressure so he's breathing down my neck now, and he won't appreciate me looking into secret societies. Especially if he's a Mason. And speak of the devil…' She held up her phone. 'Gotta go. Don't get into any trouble while I'm gone, eh?'

'Anyway,' said Darren, 'let's talk about something else, please. How did you get on with those monks, Helen? The Order of the Desert Fathers?'

'Just to point out, that's not changing the subject at all. We're talking about exactly the same thing. I don't know about the monks. There's something off about the place. And there's a novice there – younger than us, about to take vows. There's something that doesn't feel right about it. I'm going to try and find out where they lived before their current house in Blundellsands. The abbot was oddly cagey about it. There's no denying the correlation – they arrive in Liverpool in the 1600s, and shortly after, the chain of bodies begins.'

Chapter Fourteen

Darren had been right. By narrowing her Missing Persons search to the immediate area around the beach, Colette had found the Wild Woman's identity. Diane Goodwin had been a resident at Keystone House, a local half-way house for newly-released prisoners on probation, in 1995. She had been reported missing just after her departure from Keystone, after she had failed to attend a meeting with her Probation Officer. The case was eventually dropped but she had never been found. As soon as Colette saw the photo in the files, she knew it was the Wild Woman, although it was a shock to see the changes beyond the normal signs of ageing. The chin-length auburn hair in the photo had now turned to matted grey, and the pink round cheeks to sharp edges. The only similarity was the sad and slightly defiant expression in her eyes which were now sunken into their sockets.

Colette and DCI McGregor parked on the road outside Keystone House, and finished their coffees in the car.

'Nice work, Colette, tracing her here. It's not easy to find a missing person going that far back.'

'Actually, it was Darren's idea to keep the search very local. His theory was that she was from the area – that's how she knew about the Second World War bunkers.'

'You what? You talked to Darren Swift about the case?'

'Only about what was already in the public domain. He brought it up and offered the suggestion.' Colette instinctively didn't tell McGregor about Darren's vague theories on the case – that the woman had been in the area all along – and that she had maybe been underground. Darren and McGregor had always had a fraught relationship. John McGregor was a career bobby who had risen through the ranks over almost forty years of service. He swore by procedure and protocol, and was openly contemptuous of anything innovative or 'new-fangled'. So he had struggled to accept Darren, a fast-tracked young detective with fluorescent trainers and unorthodox methods. 'Anyway, he hasn't left the police for good, he's only on a sabbatical.'

'That lad doesn't do things by the book, and if you ask me, he was promoted too fast, but I'll be the first to admit he's a good detective. I hope he comes back after he gets whatever he needs to get out of his system. But in the meantime,' he handed her his empty coffee cup to dispose of as they got out of the car, 'keep your pub chats to football, yeah?'

'Can't do that with Darren - I'm an Everton supporter.'

'Jesus. I knew there was a reason I didn't like you.'

Keystone House consisted of three large Edwardian terraced houses joined together as one institution. It stood on a quiet side street just off the main shopping area on the border of Blundellsands and Crosby. They rang the doorbell under a brass plaque which stated: *At the heart of the community, through the generations.*

'Keystone House. How many times has this place changed its name?' asked McGregor as they waited. 'Last time I was here it was called Alight or something Mickey Mouse like that.'

'That's the privatisation of the prison service for you. They spend half their budget on rebranding every few years. This place provides a great service though. It's been here for centuries - it was a Christian Fellowship poor house before.'

'Yeah, considering how many ne'er-do-wells pass through here, it's impressive we don't get called out more often.'

The intercom buzzed into life. 'Hello officers, I'll be right down,' said a voice.

'What did Diane say when you mentioned this place to her?' McGregor asked Colette.

'A flicker of something, maybe. But maybe I was just imagining it. She's almost catatonic. Whoever she was, back when she lived here, she's a different person now.'

'Right, let's get this over with.'

'Just to be clear, boss, what are we investigating? I mean, as far as they are concerned?'

'We're trying to find out if a crime has been committed. There's no need for them to be worried, though, because whatever happened, happened after Diane left. They fulfilled their responsibility to her. We need to account for twenty-five years of a woman's life. It's conceivable, I suppose, that someone could disappear for that long – but no address, no bank account, no National Insurance payments - it's pretty weird. There are signs of neglect, and we need to find out if that's simply self-neglect.'

Behind the frosted glass window pane in the door they saw movement, and then the blurred smile of Supervisor Anne Matheson as she opened a series of locks.

'Come in, come in. It's quiet this time of day.'

She led them into the hallway, which was empty except for a notice board displaying posters that advertised training schemes, evening classes, addiction counselling, and a rack of leaflets on health and welfare.

Keystone House was essentially a set of bedsits with a communal lounge and dining room, plus Anne's office at the back of the house, to which she took them now.

'Come and sit yourselves down. As I say, it's quiet this time of day. Actually, we've got a quiet bunch here at the moment. Right, I've got her file – you're in luck actually, because any longer than thirty years and it would have been destroyed. We're only digitising records back to the 1990s.'

In front of her lay a red cardboard folder slightly faded with age, which she opened and read from.

'Diane Goodwin, resident here between May 1994 and April 1995 as a condition of her release from Styal Prison. It says she served five years for manslaughter. Who did she kill? I wasn't around then.'

McGregor filled her in. 'Diane Goodwin was convicted of manslaughter in 1985 for the murder of her husband Alan Goodwin. It was later reduced on appeal to manslaughter, on the grounds of evidence of prolonged domestic abuse. She served ten years of her sentence before being released on parole in 1994 and she spent a year here.'

'So, you didn't work here then?' asked Colette.

Anne mocked being offended. 'How old do you think I am? I was still in school in 1995. And most of our current staff are younger than me. But there is Tony, the caretaker. He's been here forever. Apparently, he started as a resident ex-offender here in the Seventies, and never left. So, it's possible that he remembers her. I'll go and get him, shall I?'

She began to get up, but McGregor motioned for her to remain seated. 'In a bit, that would be great, yes. But let's just go through the files first. So she was here for almost twelve months – do you have any incidents in the records that stand out? Disciplinary issues, therapy sessions, activities, comings and goings? Medication, drug use?'

'Let's see. The record-keeping wasn't quite the same back then. There're the odd prescriptions here for antidepressants, antibiotics, records of meetings with her counsellor. Nothing out of the ordinary... not until after her release, when she missed her first session with her probation officer. Never turned up at her old address. That's when she was reported as a missing person. That's the end of the file.'

'What about visitors?'

'The visitors' book is separate, but in any case, we don't have it going back as far as the 1990s.'

'Was it women only back then?'

No, it's been mixed for a long time. Because they're not prisoners any longer, and they weren't violent prisoners. But we do tend to have more women, because women are more vulnerable. When a man goes to prison, there's often a woman back home supporting him - whether it's a girlfriend or mother. But a woman tends to lose everything – her children taken into care, the man moves on, she loses the address - so they are less likely to have somewhere to go back to.'

Colette and McGregor nodded their recognition.

'Diane seems to be very religious,' Colette said. 'I notice there's a church next door, and this place used to be part of the Christian Fellowship. Do you have religious services?'

'We don't, no, this isn't a religious institution any more. But it's funny you should mention it, because we have a long relationship with this bunch of monks in Blundellsands. Lovely blokes, they are. They come in and do meditation sessions, and bring books from their library.'

'Is that the Order of the Desert Fathers, big house near the beach?'

'Yes, that's the one. Father Zotti, gorgeous Italian accent. Actually, one of our recent residents has gone off to become a monk there. Owen O'Malley. Not sure what I think about that, to be honest.'

Anne went off to get the caretaker, leaving the file for Colette and McGregor to flick through. There was the photo Colette had already seen, paperclipped to the first page, and there were two other photos, slightly sepia-toned with age. One of Diane helping out in the kitchen, smiling in an apron and hairnet, and another of her in a vegetable garden or allotment. She and another woman were wearing blue overalls, posing with their spades and plants on either side of an older man in brown workwear.

Colette skimmed through the official records on Diane from the Criminal Records Bureau.

'This was a controversial case. She killed her husband. Whether he deserved it or not, I wonder if there was someone waiting to take revenge on her when she got out.'

'Or maybe she wanted to take revenge on herself. There are prescriptions for antidepressants here, and I'm seeing the word 'guilt' crop up several times in these psychiatrist reports.'

Anne came back with the caretaker, a wizened, overly-wrinkled man who hunched in a posture of permanent apology. 'This is Tony Norris, detectives. Everyone says he really is the keystone of Keystone House, right Tony? He's forgotten more about this place than I'll ever know.'

Colette instantly recognised Tony Norris from the file – he had been the one standing next to Diane in the gardening photo. Tony Norris looked in his seventies, probably well over retirement age but with nowhere else to go. He wore jeans, a shirt and an ancient carpenter's sleeveless work jacket filled with pockets. He looked anxious and ready to be hostile and defensive as he sat down next to Anne.

'Don't worry, Mr Norris,' said McGregor, 'we're just looking into someone who lived here a long time ago.'

'What's your role here, Mr Norris?'

Tony began to speak, then looked anxiously at Anne for help.

'Tony's got a bit of a speech impediment. But he does everything here - plumbing, electrics, anything that needs fixing…'

'H… H… handyman,' Tony mumbled.

'Oh absolutely, Tony. Handyman.'

'And where do you live, Tony?'

'H… Here.'

'Do you own any other property? Allotment, lock-up?'

He looked across at Anne, and Colette wondered if he would

have lied had she not been in the room. 'I've got… an allotment and tool shed, over in Waterloo like.'

Anne placed a calming hand on Tony's knee. 'It's the association's allotment. Tony grows vegetables for our kitchen, but he also takes the residents there, helps them learn. He's very gentle with them. Quietly influential, actually.'

'Tony, do you remember Diane Goodwin?'

Tony's face had been such a picture of worry since he entered the room that it was hard to discern anything from his expression.'

'D… Diane? Don't think so.'

'You don't remember taking Diane Goodwin to the allotment? This was a very long time ago.'

Tony shook his head uncertainly.

'So, you don't remember? But you were there with her though, look.'

She showed him the photo, and he stared at it. 'Oh. Yeah.' He stared at it for so long that Anne decided to speak. 'It was such a long time ago. I'm not sure I could remember a face from the 1990s.'

But Colette ignored her. 'Tony? Can you remember anything about Diane? Did she have any visitors? Do you know where she went?'

He fiddled with his fingers in his lap, and shook his head. 'No, sorry. I don't remember anything.'

As they stepped back into the street, Colette asked McGregor:

'Do you think he knows something?'

'Hard to say. Go and check out his allotment just in case, and quickly, before he gets there himself. But given what she did, it's more likely, if someone else is involved, that is, to be someone from her family. Some sort of revenge.'

'I've started looking, but there's no close relatives left. What about those monks?'

'I suppose there must be someone there who was around in the 1990s. Worth a try. They're like old people's homes, these places nowadays, aren't they? But more importantly, you need to get started on ID-ing the skeleton from the 1990s. That bloody TV scientist is all over it, and it would be really embarrassing if the university gets there before us.'

Colette thought about Darren's theory. The 1990s skeleton was a young person who had been bludgeoned to death. By Darren's theory, this person would have disappeared, locally, in the late 80s or even 1990.

'Yeah, I'll look into it.' But she decided not to tell McGregor Darren's theory. She wasn't sure she could even find the words to describe how ridiculous it was. A series of prisoners, through the ages, who either waited patiently for death, or if their patience ran out, were bludgeoned to make way for the next. Was that the vague theory floating in all their minds, a theory they didn't dare put into words?

As they were about to get into the car, Colette decided to take a chance on something else.

'Boss, can I ask you something?'

'Depends. Go on.'

'Are you in the Masons?'

'You what?'

'The Freemasons, you know.'

'I'm in the Rotary Club, you divvy! Not the Masons! Can you see me wearing one of those Freemason costumes and doing secret handshakes? Bloody hell. You want to ask Superintendent Canter about the Masons, she's in the women's version. Quite high up I believe.'

'Is she? My god.'

'It's no secret – it's a networking thing. It's all out in the open. You've got secret societies on the brain. You should spend less time with that Darren Swift. Grab a couple of uniforms and get yourselves down to the allotments now, before Tony Norris has a chance to move anything.'

'What are you going to do?'

'I'm going to pay a visit to those monks. And after that, never you mind. I might go and do a satanic ritual. Fucking hell. The Masons.'

Chapter Fifteen

Colette surveyed the sea of allotments in front of her. Kirby Lane Allotment Association covered over ten hectares, stretching all the way from the Seaforth industrial estate to underneath the railway lines.

'Jesus. There must be hundreds of sheds here.' She, Dave and Baz contemplated the task ahead of them, from the shelter of the railway bridge. It was tipping it down, with torrential rain forecast that afternoon. The only benefit of the rain was that the place was deserted; no curious gardeners to interfere with their search.

She shielded her iPad from her wet raincoat and examined the allotment map. 'Right, the Keystone House plot is number fifty-seven, so that must be over there somewhere. But we're going to check everything. These lock-ups under the arches, too.'

'What are we looking for exactly? A shed?'

'I'm not sure, to be honest. Anything suspicious. A building that looks out of place.'

'There's no way you could lock someone in a shed for even a day, people would hear them.'

'Unless that person wanted to be there.'

'That's true, yeah.'

As they moved from plot to plot, examining innocent tool sheds, peering through the windows of greenhouses whose windows were clouded by condensation, Colette thought about Darren. She trusted him completely, and yet she had the strange feeling that he only ever told her half the story. And that, somehow, it had to be that way. That perhaps there were things she was not supposed to know. It was weird. Could it really be possible, that someone would have themselves voluntarily imprisoned, for decades, and that it could have been going on for centuries? And the ones who changed their minds or tried to escape were killed?

It happened. You did hear about these cases; they would surface once in a while. That man in Austria, what was his name, who kept a specially prepared cellar in his own house and kept half his family down there in semi-darkness. His daughter survived down there for over twenty years, didn't she? That guy in America who kept three girls prisoner for ten years. And then that other guy… In fact, she could think of multiple cases, because they all made the international press. Everyone wanted to read about these cases, those real-life houses of horror, with a sort of prurient curiosity, as it played into their deepest fears – the fear of being buried alive. How could someone do that to another person? And how could it go on for so long? What was really happening behind closed doors on neighbourhood streets?

The scariest ones were the cases where the victim was willing. Patty Hearst, was that her name, the famous one? And all those religious cults. Stockholm Syndrome, everyone had heard of that, when captives begin to identify with their captors and become complicit. And according to Darren's theory, Diane Goodwin may have been a willing victim.

They found plot fifty-seven, which was quadruple the size of most of the others. Tony Norris was clearly green-fingered, and had put the centre's land to great use. There were rows of thriving vegetable crops, lush clumps of herbs and lettuce, giant sunflowers, and an area covered with plastic under which were hundreds of tomato plants. The colour of this plot alone made it stand out; the rest of the allotment looked drab by comparison.

'It's like the place has its own tiny micro-climate,' said Baz.

'Are they miniature gravestones?' Colette moved over to an area of grass adjacent to the vegetables, where little wooden crosses and stone plaques had been erected. There was one fresh area of newly-turned soil.

'Hey, mate!' Dave shouted to a bedraggled figure he saw back at the railway arches, a figure who darted away on being spotted.

'That's him, that's Tony Norris,' shouted Colette, and all three officers gave chase, splashing through muddy puddles and darting over plots. It didn't take long, as Tony was old and limped heavily, his right hip betraying him. All four of them hunched over to catch their breath.

'P... please, please... don't tell Anne,' he said quietly, unable to make eye contact with anyone.

'Tell Anne what? What's been going on out here?'

'He had a sideline burying dogs and cats,' Colette explained to McGregor later at the station. 'You know, when people's pets die and they don't want to pay the vet to dispose of the body.'

'So they give them to Tony instead. Is that why that place has such fertile soil? Fucking weird.'

'God yes, that's creepy isn't it. He was giving them all proper burials, little gravestones. I don't think he understood that it's a serious health hazard, otherwise he would have covered it up.'

'It's our duty to report it, unfortunately. I feel sorry for him in a way.'

At home, Darren was also looking into graves. He tried to keep reminding himself of Occam's Razor, and that the simplest explanation for the skeletons had to be something vaguely rational. Cemeteries did have to be demolished and re-used. What if someone had just, for whatever reason, nicked some bodies? Liverpool and its surroundings had a multitude of crematoria and cemeteries. His research gave him the image of the city as one giant ossuary or necropolis, continually disposing of its dead, churning the land with corpses. Once in a while his search would fall on Sandhills Cemetery, where Matt was buried, and he tried to block it out. He visited, once a week at first, less now. He would meet Matt's mum there, and they would go back and have Caribbean food and she would remind him that Matt would have wanted him to move on... and he would wince inwardly at the thought that perhaps he already had.

It turned out that there was a well-established precedent for decommissioning cemeteries in Liverpool and turning them into parkland. Interestingly, in the past it had been more acceptable than it was now to re-use cemeteries. People had become more superstitious about it, keener to keep a buffer between the living and the dead. Even though paradoxically, with more people being cremated nowadays it was less of an issue.

But there had been no cemetery change of use or reinterments registered in the area since 1985 – which cancelled out the Sniggery Skeletons with their 1990s body.

Darren considered the possibility of a private family tomb. Was that even allowed, unregistered private burials? He made a note to ask Colette if the police might have those sorts of records. There was also the possibility of grave-robbing, or body snatching. Did that even happen? *Stranger things...* he thought. It was a horrible thought, disturbing the dead, but apparently, according to the Google wormhole he went down, 'resurrection men' were still very common in Asia, where an estimated 25,000 skeletons every year were smuggled out of India, Nepal and Bangladesh for use in mostly Western medical laboratories.

Either way, whoever had those bones had dumped them suddenly and carelessly, which implied that their storage place was about to be disturbed. Something had suddenly agitated someone into action. Something out of their control. With the familiar furtive feeling of guilt that what he was doing could be completely pointless and absurd, Darren looked up the register of planning applications. Perhaps something would stand out. The last time he had looked at this register, he had been investigating Shawn Forrest. Lover of Justine, father of Alfie, murderer of Matt, local kingpin; for whom manipulation of city planning regulations was part of his day-to-day business operations.

Even within the area local to Blundellsands, there were hundreds of planning applications – extensions, loft conversions, swimming pools. But he needed to look for something that an owner themselves could not control, or something that would affect a neighbouring property. And anyway, who could say whether any of it was potentially relevant? Could he possibly narrow it down?

This is hopeless, he thought. He looked at his pile of books about medieval hermits and anchoresses, histories of the Reformation, Stockholm syndrome. And his notice board, filled with scribbled Post-It notes about Latin phrases and skeletons. He looked at the text which had just flashed up on his phone screen from Thomas:

You can come over tonight, but make it after 10.30 to be sure the babysitter has left.

What have I done? What am I doing?

He felt himself in a sort of purgatory, where reality had disintegrated and was re-pixelating itself effortlessly, that he could take control of it if he wanted and yet he felt no compulsion to add his own input. Only a strange passivity and a mild dread.

Helen was also sitting at her desk, engaged in research that was tangential to almost everything, and yet felt more important than anything. From her top floor flat on New Hope Street, she could see the Anglican cathedral and its catacombs lit up in the darkness. She was looking through the New Testament which she knew almost off by heart, and the Old Testament which she knew far less well, for clues about - about what? Imprisonment, human sacrifice, martyrdom… In some ways the whole Bible was about those subjects. But the Bible only told one part of the story.

She noted, once again, that the God of the Old Testament was not a benevolent God. And the crucifixion made no sense if people were to believe that God is a benevolent God. But the story of the New Testament was something different. The narrative changed - did the Church fathers decide to make a benevolent God? Even atheists had this idea that God was kind and benign. But where did this idea really come from? It was an incredible spin, really. Well, she supposed that a series of absurdities could sometimes lead one to the truth.

Mikko was laid back on the sofa strumming an old electric guitar he had picked up in a charity shop. He looked aimless, dreamy, but once in a while he would mouth lyrics and stare into space in concentration as he picked out a riff, as if he might be half-composing something. Helen wondered if she should buy him an amplifier, or if perhaps he might be offended at her presumption. She felt that she had trapped him here in a sort of limbo, lying like a log across his path. He couldn't possibly spend half his life travelling and then the other half camped out here, still far from home. But whenever she suggested he might want to go home to Norway he became irritated. 'You don't have to push me away,' he would say. 'You are allowed not to. It's not a bad thing to want me here. Stop trying to find reasons not to be happy.'

How exhausting relationships were. Having to constantly guess the other's horizon of thought. As a nun she had been so rigorously trained to keep her feelings at arm's length, to live without earthly love, to reject human affection; it was supposed to be a training to last a lifetime. Nuns were not supposed to dismantle their prisons and go back out into the world, lay themselves open to falling in love and being fallen in love with. Mikko's patience with her was endless as she tried to overcome her repression. *Stop trying to find reasons not to be happy.* Yes, that's exactly what she was doing. Because she didn't deserve to be happy.

Helen noticed that Mikko's strumming had become more sporadic, because he was sending texts and receiving texts back, smiling and nodding to himself. Finally, his phone rang and he picked up a video call. She noticed her pang of jealousy at the look of pleasure on his face, then her feeling of relief when she heard that it was a man's voice.

'Jared, good to see you, man!'

The rich, gentle tones of the handsome evangelical came through the phone, flooded the room, his charisma not dulled by the phone interference. After a couple of minutes of bantering with each other, Mikko said 'I'm gonna take this in the bedroom, so I don't disturb Helen,' and he signalled vaguely to her as he took the phone away to continue the conversation behind a closed door.

But Helen found herself disturbed. She could no longer concentrate on her books. She found Jared Case a little insipid, inauthentic. His aura of all-encompassing kindness was hard to buy. She tried to define her slight unease - was it guilt that Mikko was so bored here that he had befriended someone with whom he had nothing in common? It didn't make any sense, and she had a slightly darker worry. Were Total Depravity planning some stunt at this festival? What was this enthusiasm to play a Christian metal gig in the north of England when they were supposed to be resting before the real festival season began? How well did she really know Mikko? He had certainly been a little withdrawn recently.

Eventually Mikko came back into the room, and she heard

Lamb of God

Jared saying 'Alright brother, god bless you,' before Mikko switched off his phone and jumped back onto the sofa to pick up his guitar. *Is he avoiding my gaze?* She couldn't help herself, and put down her pencil. 'You two sound as if you've known each other forever.'

'Yeah, I guess in a way it feels like that. He's a good guy.'

'For an evangelical Christian.'

'Right.'

'I'm worried. They are a sort of cult, after all. The Guardians Of Truth.'

'Depends on your definition of a cult. The whole of Christianity is a cult.'

'What if they are setting you up?'

'What if we are setting them up?'

'Are you?'

'Have a little faith in me, will you.'

He said it with a smiling nonchalance that was designed to diffuse all tension, but she felt it anyway, a tension she couldn't define. Intimacy was such hard work, and they were so very different. She had no idea whether he was happy to play his guitar or whether he wanted her full attention. And her attention was distracted by the mystery of the Wild Woman. Helen wished she could just go and talk to this woman in hospital; she felt sure they would have a connection. But she knew it wouldn't be impossible, even if Darren was still in the police. The last time he had involved her in an investigation, by allowing her to see the inside of Andrew Shepherd's apartment, he had almost lost his job for bringing an outsider to a crime scene.

There had to be an explanation. Helen was beginning to have a suspicion that the entire history of Christianity was a history of trying to explain away ridiculous ideas. It was like political spin. She was starting to see the desperate zeal and creativity of the human mind in finding endless solutions to stories that could not possibly be true. Or could they?

She surveyed her books. The Sayings of the Desert Fathers, The Complete Apocrypha, The Confessions of St Augustine. Somewhere amidst this esoterica, these apocryphal works that didn't make it into the Bible, she felt sure there was a text that could explain the Wild Woman's story. The problem was that the majority of apocryphal works hadn't even been discovered yet; they were still buried in ancient tombs in the Middle East or, more likely, already ground into dust. As she looked into more esoteric things, she was looking for a more personal relationship with God, and struggling to find it. Maybe amongst all of it, she could find answers not just to the Wild Woman's mystery, but to her own.

Have a little faith. Not long ago, her faith was the only thing she could be sure about. Now a terrifying notion was creeping up on her - the notion that she might be losing her faith altogether.

Chapter Sixteen

Rain lashed against the window, as Diane Goodwin looked out at the hospital car park. For the first few days, the curtains had remained closed, and every time the door was opened by some doctor or nurse or police officer she jumped with fright. Now she could cope with the light, it no longer terrified her or hurt her eyes, and she was beginning to relax into watching the world go by. And the world still turned; cars came and went, the sun rose and set, the weather changed, clouds and birds moved across the sky. And although she still jumped every time the door opened, they had not come for her, so the anchor must be holding.

When she had been there, down there, sometimes she would hear children's laughter, a dog barking, a seagull, little else. And she wanted them to come close, yet didn't want them to. Sometimes a distant car alarm, siren, even a foghorn out at sea, or an overhead plane diverted from its usual flightpath. These were the shadows of sounds that marked her day. At night she would wait underneath the entrance. She had long learned not to scream there, but at least she could be ready to catch a glimpse of stars when it opened, even a blast of cold air or gust of wind. The constellations would move gradually so that she could feel the turning of the earth, and buried there she was part of that turning. She had created her own concept of time. Learning to make the intolerable tolerable was her only occupation, her strength and her joy.

The sight of people coming and going outside in the hospital car park still aroused involuntary panic, but she began to look with some curiosity. Cars were different now, sleeker somehow, but not the futuristic caricatures she might have imagined. Everything was technicolour, but no more so than she remembered. Perhaps the present was always more technicolour than the past. People did not dress so differently, but they seemed to be under the control of small devices, miniature computers that they held in front of them and stared into, tapped at, and she wondered if it was some monitoring system. Some change in government or revolution that she had missed. But other than that, everything looked the same. If she was in Hell, or the waiting room of Hell, she had been here before.

Had things changed so much, or did she just not remember what it was like before? In the old world. Before. Yesterday they had finally told her it had been twenty-nine years. She was not shocked, only numb. Because time moved differently down there, so that twenty-nine years meant both forever and no time at all.

She looked at her wasted legs and moved her toes, which were now clean and recognisable. She curled them and watched them move, in mild fascination that these were her own limbs she was controlling. Someone had come and bathed her feet, and she had flinched in automatic terror, as she had at all their touches. But the touch had been kind and the memory of kindness had sparked some recognition. And perhaps it was right, appropriate, that someone should wash her feet, the martyr's feet. Or perhaps she should be the one washing their feet. In imitation of Christ.

They had given her a mirror, a hand mirror, and at first it had been an object of terror, and her face an object of disgust, with its ghostly pallor, rotten teeth, and wrinkles. Now she looked at herself with curiosity. Fragments of memory beginning to piece together a new selfhood. She fingered the necklace that she had worn all this time, faded now from all her touch but still a red colour of sorts. A memory of a red colour.

Confusion reigned; some days she thought this was yet another waiting room in purgatory, other days that she truly had risen. They had not come for her. Why had they not come? The flowers and cards were all from strange well-wishers who had heard her story. The nurse had even shown her picture in the newspaper. Had the chain been broken, or had it already been taken up by someone else?

The young nurse knocked and opened, bursting in with the constructed breeziness that Diane had begun to realise was part of her treatment. Barely more than a child, yet this nurse took her in hand like she was an old lady. Perhaps she was an old lady. She had to keep reminding herself that she and the nurse were not the same age. Words like rehabilitation, recovery, re-entry were being used. Maybe it was possible. Redemption.

'Hello Diane! I just wanted to show you these – look how beautiful they are! Spring flowers are my favourite. To your real name, I mean. Someone who knows you! She held a ceramic pot filled with an array of spring flowers, daffodils, bluebells, snowdrops, and primroses. The bulbs bulged out of the soil.

'I'm sorry, love, but you know we have to open everything, just to check. It doesn't say who it's from but it must be someone who knows you. And there's a message. I don't know what this means though. Do you?'

Diane was confronted with a large pot of spring flowers - crocuses, daffodils, tulips, bluebells. It was so beautiful it brought tears to her eyes. She had not seen flowers like this for such a long time. In the middle of the flowers was placed a white envelope, with 'Diane Goodwin' printed on the front in red type.

Balancing the pot on her knees, she opened the envelope, its seal already broken, and looked at the card inside. And all the hopes and frail possibilities came crashing down. The spring flowers were cruel. April was the cruelest month - where had she heard that before? The anchor did not hold.

Cast thyself into the bottomless pit and set a seal upon it, that you shall deceive nations no more. If you fail, you shall end your life with a thorn to the heart, as the thorns that pierced my Son.

She recited the words she had recited so many times before, just to hear the sound of her own voice. And she remarked, even at the moment before her death, how different her voice sounded in this new room

Cover thyself in darkness and abide there forever.

She held the pot lightly, touched the flowers lightly, ran her fingertips down their leaves and stems. Leaned forward to sniff their fresh, crisp sweetness. She would have liked to taste the outdoors again, just once. But it was too late. She had been reminded – and how dare she forget – that fate depended on her continued martyrdom.

She dug her fingers into the soil, the dirt under her fingernails again the way they had been before. As she had dug her own grave. And soon her fingers struck something buried. There it was.

When the nurse returned an hour later, her screams echoed down the corridor.

Chapter Seventeen

Darren had warned Helen to stay away from the monks. It was unthinkable that they could be involved with this, but if the unthinkable happened to be true, and they were somehow involved, Helen - as a lapsed nun - would be regarded as something of an enemy to them. Certainly, a candidate for atonement.

But like the proverbial moth, Helen had been unable to resist, and here was Father Zotti standing behind the lectern in her lecture theatre, in his cream-coloured robes and wooden cross, smiling benignly at a sea of student faces as she introduced him.

'And so, continuing our guest-speaker series of local religious leaders' - Helen hoped the class wouldn't notice that she had no such series, but was now determined to start one since it was actually a good idea - 'I'm very pleased to welcome Father Angelo Zotti, the abbot of Belmont House, home of the Liverpool chapter of the Order Of The Desert Fathers. He's going to tell us about the history of the order, their lives here in Liverpool, and something about the desert fathers, their beliefs and sacred texts. And there'll be plenty of time for questions at the end.'

Father Zotti's face showed a momentary flicker of concern, before he turned it into a joke 'uh-oh' grimace to the audience. Helen hadn't actually told him anything about the content of the afternoon. She had been deliberately vague, ignoring the voice telling her how unprofessional she was being. Whatever he had been planning to talk about, she was determined to catch him off guard.

'Thank you very much, Dr. Hope, it's a great pleasure to be here and to address such a young audience interested in theology. Although I must admit I am not very well-prepared, I will try to give you a little insight into the life of a modern monk. So, what is a desert father, and why are we named after them?

'The earliest Christian monks inhabited the desert land of the Middle East starting at the end of the second century AD. Known as the "Desert Fathers", they left everything in search of knowing Jesus Christ by making the Gospels absolutely integral to their daily lives. They wanted to commit themselves totally - body, soul, mind, and will - to being disciples of the Lord Jesus, with a profound holy zeal moving them to become ever more like Christ. These monks practised integrity of character with an unrelenting courage, that required their whole being to remain in the state of constant humility that comes from knowing that they were loved by God. Paradoxically, their extraordinarily harsh penances often resulted in gentleness and patience towards others, especially other monks, but also visitors who came seeking an understanding of the essence of spiritual life. These monks sought, most of all, to experience union with God in the quiet of the desert and in the silence of their hearts.'

He paused and smiled. 'And we have found a desert of our own with Crosby Beach.'

Darren was sitting in the middle row, pen poised, and he raised his hand. 'Were you near the beach in the seventeenth century as well? I believe the current house was built in the nineteenth century. Sorry, I'm just interested in the architecture of the area, because there wasn't much near the beach until the shipping merchants started building the big houses there.'

'I'm afraid you've got me there, and Dr. Hope asked me the same question a couple of weeks ago. I haven't had a chance to find out, and you're right, I certainly should know. I will consult our records.'

'Thanks,' Darren nodded, and briefly met Helen's eyes. She had told him to ask about where the Order had resided before Belmont House; she couldn't ask it again, and she knew Father Zotti would give the same non-committal answer, but she wanted him to squirm. Emboldened by dislike and suspicion, she found herself leaning back in her chair at the side of the stage, arms folded in a sceptical pose that was very unlike her.

'I have a question, Father Zotti,' she said. 'Many of the apocrypha were attributed to the desert fathers. Are there any writers that you subscribe to in particular?'

'Well, the best-known desert father, the founding father if you like, was St Anthony The Great. He was one of life's permanent outsiders, and rather enjoyed the fact that Christianity was outlawed by the Romans. So, when the Roman Empire legalized Christianity in 313, it gave Anthony a greater resolve to go out into the desert. Nostalgic for the tradition of martyrdom, St Anthony saw withdrawal and asceticism as an alternative.'

'Are you nostalgic for the tradition of martyrdom, Father Zotti?' She asked with such theatrical academic faux-innocence that the audience could not fail to pick up on the tension between the two of them.

'Martyrdom, no. But sacrifice, now that is something we should all consider. Sacrifice becomes a beautiful thing. We must all be imitators of Christ, in this world that worships consumerism. And so, we are quite radical, in that respect. Christ devoted his life to kindness, to teaching, to the care of others. And then he gave his life, at the age of only thirty-three, still a young man with no family, in order to save others. We must all try to be a little more Christ-like.'

'I have another question,' said Helen, not even looking at him this time, but at the audience. 'The desert fathers, wandering free through the wilderness. Surely it's the opposite of the enclosed life?'

He betrayed a momentary withering expression, because he knew that she knew the answer to this, knew that she was just being provocative. If someone had asked her this question even two years ago, she would have answered exactly the same as Father Zotti. 'It's about spiritual wilderness,' he said, also addressing the audience instead of her. 'The desert is a metaphor. As you know. Another of the desert fathers, Abba Moses, said "Sit in thy cell and thy cell will teach thee all." We seek complete solitude – real solitude – without the distractions of modern life. It's very difficult to be a hermit nowadays.'

Helen folded her arms. 'I would disagree. Some might say we are all more isolated than ever.'

'Then surely that is an argument for our continued relevance,' said Father Zotti, his voice betraying a combative position now.

There were sharp intakes of breath around the room. No student would ask a question now, they were focused on the personal drama unfolding between their lecturer and her guest. Helen decided to pull back before she went too far, but the rest of the session passed awkwardly.

After the lecture, as the students filed out, Helen invited Father Zotti for a coffee, but he declined. 'I think we've probably had quite enough of each other now, don't you? You certainly put me on the spot in there, Helen. I'm rather tired now.'

He headed up the stairs towards the door at the back of the theatre, but Helen followed, not having finished with him. 'I'm sorry if we grilled you. It's just such a fascinating subject. I was actually hoping that your new novice - Owen is it? I thought he might have accompanied you.'

Father Zotti put his head to one side benignly. 'Why?'

'I don't know, really. I just thought it might be interesting for him. And for our students. You know, a young person making that sort of a choice is very unusual.'

'You've said that before. And I've said before that it's not so unusual. Owen is busy preparing for his ordination ceremony. He will be doing two weeks of solitary confinement now until Easter.'

'Solitary confinement. Right.' Helen could not hide her expression.

'Look, Dr. Hope.' Now he had returned to addressing her formally, his method of conveying hostility. 'You don't need to worry about Owen. He's not a boy, he's a grown man of thirty-three. He's the same age as you. Don't you feel old enough to make your own choices? He committed terrible crimes in his life and now he is repenting. Let him. We are taking good care of him. He is free to leave at any point, but he chooses not to. He has found sanctuary with us.'

'I just...'

'He's an informed adult, Dr. Hope. And he is weary of this world. People who carry a burden like his need spiritual help that we can provide. Now please excuse me.'

Darren appeared at Helen's side. They were the only people left in the theatre now as Father Zotti nodded to them both coldly and edged his way out.

'How does he know your age?' asked Darren.

'I suppose he could have guessed.'

'But it's an odd thing to say though, isn't it?'

Helen had winced inwardly when Zotti had mentioned her age. She didn't feel thirty-three, and that ticking biological clock somewhere deep inside was making her feel irritable with the beginnings of a chronic low-level panic.

Chapter Eighteen

'The knife was buried in the soil.'

Colette and DCI McGregor stood at the end of Diane Goodwin's bed as the police photographer snapped. Dodging to and fro to get out of the way, eventually they stepped back to the doorway.

Diane's body lay almost flat, but her head was propped on the pillow, eyes open in terror and looking straight ahead. The hands which had plunged the knife into her chest had fallen to either side of her. Blood had poured in rivers down each arm and dripped into large pools on the floor. Her necklace no longer looked red at all, its colour pale in comparison to the deep crimson liquid.

'Is it really possible to stab yourself to death?' Colette asked. She tried to imagine someone raising a knife above their own chest, lining up the point so the blade would strike in exactly the right place, taking a deep breath, making the single movement with sufficient force. She found herself automatically mimicking the action. Could someone really do that? Or would they need help?

'I've never heard of it,' shrugged McGregor. 'But Colvin should be here in a minute, and he's seen everything there is to see, so maybe he can tell us.'

'In any case, we've already got the CCTV from the corridor. Nobody came in or out apart from the nurse, so it appears to be a clear-cut suicide.'

'How did she know to look in the soil for the knife?'

The plant pot had been placed on Diane's side table, but the bulbs had been torn out and there was soil on the bed sheets and the floor where she had pulled out the knife.

'The message in the card must have meant something to her.'

With the photos now taken, Colette put on gloves and placed the card, only the size of a business card, in a clear evidence bag. The greeting message had been typed in red italic font:

Vade in pacem.

'That means go in peace, in Latin, right? Let me check.' She tapped into her phone. 'Yep. How do you get from 'go in peace' to 'stab yourself in the chest?''

Pathologist Dr. Colvin arrived, tweeds covered by hazmat suit.

'Well, well.' He managed to temper his glee at the pathological puzzle before him with the appropriate amount of gravitas and solemnity. 'Detective Sergeant Quinn, what on earth have you brought me this time?' He walked around the bed in fascination.

'Before you get started, Dr. Colvin, quick question. Is it even possible to stab yourself to death?'

He peered at the wound over the top of his glasses, then looked back at them.

'Possible, yes. With knowledge. Very rare in a woman though. Self-stabbing was regarded as an honourable death in Japanese warrior culture. For men it was called seppuku, and involved stabbing in the abdomen, but required assistance. For women it was called jigai, and could be done alone - but it involved cutting the jugular vein.' Colvin made a slashing motion at his neck. 'Self-stabbing in the heart is extremely rare. It's certainly not the easy choice, but probably the only option in this place. It's a psychiatric ward.' He looked around the room. 'No hooks for hanging, electrics set to cut out at the slightest tampering, unbreakable window glass, no access to drugs. And fifteen-minute checks, so slitting your wrists is too slow.'

'So that's why she stabbed herself. To make sure that she died. She knew how to survive in the wild, and how to die in captivity too, it seems.'

Colvin moved around the body muttering into his dictaphone. 'Three centimetre stab wound to the left thoracic region... all chambers of the heart empty... Three hesitation marks followed by single incision... Stab channel through third intercostal... death by exsanguination...'

'Right, shall we go and interview the nurse then?' The officers stepped outside the room into the corridor, where there were anxious murmurs from hospital staff gathered in clusters.

'Yeah. The hospital is assembling lawyers, they're worried about negligence. But I'm not sure there's anything they could have done. Who delivered the flowers?'

'The flowers were delivered by a van from MyFlowers – it's one of those central delivery services that all the florists use - so the key is to find out who made that order.'

'I'll get on that as soon as we're done here. It shouldn't be too hard to find out who bought those flowers. MyFlowers will have the records.'

They stopped just outside the doorway, inside the police line, to take one more look at Diane's body.

'Boss,' said Colette. 'What is this investigation now?'

'What d'you mean?'

'Well, it's not murder, is it?'

'Probably not, but incitement to suicide is a serious crime. Did someone help her to die, or compel her to die?'

'It's dead weird. It's like she knew exactly what to do. And to find that strength. It's like she became something other than human. Something super-human.' *Like an angel, or a devil*, she found herself thinking.

'Either way, this escalates the investigation. If someone went to the trouble of killing Diane Goodwin, they could do the same again. She knew something. They needed her to die before she started speaking. We need to hurry.'

Chapter Nineteen

They tramped through woodland, fingers lightly touching, a soft carpet of last year's rotted acorns beneath their feet. They had long strayed from the main trail and were following vague desire paths deeper into the woods. Occasionally they moved into single file to avoid clumps of nettles or to hold back brambles and branches for each other. Only March but it was already t-shirt weather, and the shafts of sunlight dappled the skin on her bare arms, showed nothing against his thick covering of tattoos.

The birdsong was a chorus of incessant cheerfulness, yet Helen's mind was filled with thoughts of atonement, sacrifice and imprisonment, and she was quite happy about it. This was a theological puzzle so delicious she could almost have set it as a class assignment. And indeed, she wasn't completely sure she hadn't invented it herself. What sort of a religious sect would involve a person being permanently enclosed? It was of course an extreme form of monasticism, and she couldn't help but think it sounded exactly like anchorites and anchoresses. The pattern fit, there was no denying it.

And people did all sorts of things in the name of religion. In the name of atonement. She had offered herself as a living sacrifice, in order to atone for her brother's death. Was this just an extreme version of what she did? Her mood darkened as she thought of Owen the novice. She had to do something to save him.

Every monastic order had its own sacred texts. Her own order swore by Calvin's Institutes of the Christian Religion, which were themselves influenced by the writings of St Augustine of Hippo.

Lamb of God

She had been through the books of the Bible that mentioned sacrifice. And there were of course the apocrypha too, and then the texts that had not yet been found, may never be found. So, what did the Order of the Desert Fathers believe? If she could identify their sacred texts, it might provide a clue to what would happen to Owen.

She became aware that Mikko had been texting constantly, and tempered her mild irritation by reminding herself that he was perhaps simply giving her the headspace for her reverie.

'Who are you texting?' she asked finally.

'Oh, Jared.' He sent off a message, smiled at the response, then put his phone in his pocket.

'What, Jared Case again?'

'Yeah, just organising details for the festival. He's actually an ok guy.'

'An ok guy? He is the last person I could ever have imagined you calling an ok guy. I'm still confused about the level of irony on which we're attending this festival.'

'What are the different levels of irony then?'

'Irony means I'm joking. Post-irony means I'm joking to disguise the fact that I might be serious. Post-post-irony means I might be joking, or I might be serious, but it doesn't matter because you are too inferior to understand my motives.'

'Man, that sounds like something Darren's new friend James Absalom would say. He went to another one of those weird-ass debates last night, you know. I checked out the livestream. If Darren's famous footballer treated him like a proper boyfriend, instead of this shameful secret, he might have less time to spend at those events.'

'You really care about Darren, don't you? And what did you think of Absalom?'

'I don't know. He seems like… a bit of a dick. All those words.

People call him erudite. I call it lazy-ass fake intellectualism. I call bullshit. I mean, there's no doubt he's smart. He's got himself into this position where he questions everyone and everything, but no-one is allowed to question him. Like, what did he do to become head of this society?'

'It does seem as if he changes his beliefs according to convenience. And that is the ultimate cynicism.'

'Cynicism and irony are safe, lazy. Hope is dangerous. To hope, you have to open the door to disappointment, rejection, disbelief.'

'Is it really you, criticising cynicism?' She said it playfully, but he shrugged.

'Maybe I've changed. You have to be willing to throw your whole life away for something you believe is right. And I can't see him doing that.'

She felt a tension that she couldn't define. What did he mean? That she should be willing to throw away her career and follow him to Norway, follow him and his band around the world? Having spent ten years in total surrender to a group of severe old women, she now felt herself obliged to surrender herself to someone she actually loved, and bizarrely it was more difficult. Because there could be none of the delicious indignation of martyrdom here, not when she more than half-wanted to surrender herself.

They were a couple of miles inland from the coast, and the sand, pine and gorse had transformed into deciduous woodland, hedgerows. Waterways were no longer estuary and salt marsh, but canal and stream. The wind no longer battered at your eardrums, but seeped into your veins in tendrils through the gaps in your clothes. It felt more permanent, and just as unnerving.

The trees had been petering out, and Helen broke the silence by saying 'Somewhere around here there should be… yes, here it is! My goodness.' They had to squint in the sunlight again as they trampled over the last bushes and came out into a grassy clearing. In front of them in the hazy light was a series of ruined buildings. The scene was almost a caricature of a gothic rural idyll, so much so that there was an ethereal sheen over everything, a slight mist of age. Helen felt as if they had been transported into a nineteenth century painting, and it was quite magical and romantic.

'All this time it's been here, and I never knew. I can't believe I haven't been here,' she said, thinking about all the other things on which she had missed out, things which had been within her grasp all along. And now they were there for the taking, it was terrifying and she wasn't sure she wanted them.

'This place is fucking cool,' he said.

'Yes, it is.'

She had got used to his platitudes. She knew what was behind them, and somehow, he managed to encapsulate everything. It was, indeed, *fucking cool*, she supposed. It was quite magical. There was a tumbled-down Elizabethan manor house of local red brick, and in the same russet hue a crumbled church, its spire still half-intact but its bell fallen and rusted into the land. These were listed buildings but did not appear in any of the Liverpool guide books, and only the most obscure of the local histories. Someone seemed to want to keep it all as secret as possible, and she found that irresistible. Human intrusion was a rarity here, evidenced by the ivy and root tendrils that crept up the red-brick edifices, the clumps of grass that grew on top of fallen walls and rubble. Ineffaceable, and yet somehow the whole place reeked of the forgotten. It was frozen in time.

'How can this be the first time you have been here?' asked Mikko, leaping onto a foundation stone. 'We can't be more than five miles from your convent.'

'I know, and it's strange, because this is the sort of place I love. It seems rather arbitrary, the places that become celebrated and the places that are forgotten. All the stories that haven't been told, that should have been told. Alternative histories that could have been written.'

'Maybe not arbitrary. Maybe it's been kept hidden on purpose. So, what are we doing here?'

'I'm not exactly sure. This was the home of the Lunt family in the sixteenth and seventeenth centuries. They were the sort of ruling family of Crosby. That was their manor house, this their private chapel. They say there's a priest tunnel running between the two. I don't know if that's true, but this was certainly a centre of recusancy.'

'So, the Lunts remained Catholics after the Reformation?'

'Yes, exactly, lots of families did around here, and it was incredibly dangerous - punishable by torture and death. But nevertheless, the Lunt family were well-known recusants. They invited the Order of the Desert Fathers here to minister Catholic services to them in secret, and so that abbey over there,' she pointed to the church building, 'was their first home in England.'

'And what are you looking for exactly?'

'I'm not sure. I'm just trying to imagine...' What was she trying to imagine? She tried to imagine a family risking torture and death just in order to pray the way they wanted to. Trying to keep the magic of ritual alive in the face of a new and austere, unforgiving form of religion.

'How long has this place been a ruin?' he asked, touching the crumbling bricks as they rounded a wall.

'Apparently since the 1820s. And I imagine that's when the Order moved to their current home near the beach in Blundellsands. Now if we look carefully, apparently we can find evidence of a priest hole...'

Suddenly she felt herself grabbed from behind, swung around and pushed lightly against the manor wall.

'I am so goddamn attracted to you when you get all research and academic.' He pressed himself against her and she felt herself relax and allow the tension to melt into a different kind of tension. She pushed him playfully, and he pulled her back into an embrace. 'So, tell me again about these priest holes,' he whispered. 'And do it in your nun voice.'

Helen rolled her eyes. 'Ok, well in 1596...'

But he stopped her mouth with a kiss. And then said,

'You know what I'm thinking?'

'What?'

'This would be the perfect place to make a death metal video.'

She had been hoping, fearing, he would say something about their future. Because what were the possibilities? He spent more than half the year travelling. Even if he lived in Liverpool, would that be enough? But he didn't. How did people talk about these things, these fundamental things? It was too big, too much. Anyway, yet again he had terminated a serious moment with a joke.

'Yes, it would,' she said, looking around them. 'I can just imagine Anders drumming on top of that pile of bricks, and Knut attempting to set fire to the steeple.'

They wandered in and out of the fragmented structures of the manor house, making out the floor plan of a great hall, other rooms. Then they walked across the grass towards the ruined church. Helen kicked about in the grass.

'Are you looking for something in particular?'

'No. Yes. Maybe. Look at this.'

Almost obscured by thick nettles was a rusted iron disc, slightly raised off the ground.

'Isn't that just a well? A storm drain or whatever?'

'Maybe. But why would a storm drain be here, on higher ground? And why is there a well, when the river is a hundred metres over there?' She knelt down in the foliage and touched the bevelled surface of the iron disc. It had a large screw top which was far too damaged by rust to ever be opened. She rubbed at some lettering that ringed the edge of the circle, covering her hands in damp moss, soil, and lichen.

'What does it say?' Mikko peered over her shoulder.

'It says *Si vult intrare, intret*. It means 'If she wants to go in, let her go in. It was a part of the anchoress initiation ceremony. The bishop would say it before she entered and they blocked up the entrance, to signify that she was doing this of her own free will.'

'So, this is…'

'I think it's an oubliette. I wonder. I wonder.'

'You just shivered. Shall we go back in the sunlight?'

'No, it was more of a shudder. Something passing over my grave. Immurement was a punishment for nuns who broke their vows. If this was the seventeenth century, I would have been buried alive in a place like this.'

'I would have been burned at the stake long before you.'

They were standing directly on top of the oubliette now, and he put his arms around her. 'It wouldn't be so bad to be - what's it called - immured? To be immured with you.'

'That's the most romantic thing anyone has ever said to me. Let's be buried alive together.'

She leaned back in their embrace to look at him. They were exactly the same height, and had exactly the same length hair, his pale straw blond and hers jet black. Amongst the debris of tattoos around his neck there were always several necklaces; he wore his jewellery, accessories and tattoos like armour against the outside world. Her arms between his, she fingered the jumble of leather thongs and metal chains around his neck, some of which culminated in a pile of pendants at his throat and chest. And here was a new one, a red woven thread with a simple clasp.

'What's this?'

He lowered his chin to look at it. 'Oh, that - it's new. Jared gave it to me. It's like, the festival VIP pass, apparently."

'Already? When did you see him?'

'When you were teaching the other day - he was in Liverpool and we had lunch.' He looked a little put out, and she cursed herself for questioning him. But something was weird. Of course, he wasn't obliged to fill her in on his movements while she left him all day to go to work, but why would he not have mentioned that to her?

'Do you know what it means, the scarlet thread?' she asked.

'Yeah, it's the festival pass, like I said.'

'No, it's very symbolic in Christianity. Jared Case would know that. The idea is that something has to die to make a scarlet thread; originally the colour was made from the crushed bodies of pregnant crimson worms.'

'Ok, well that's fucking cool then - death and worm foetuses.'

'No, it's more than that,' she persisted. 'The scapegoat that carried sin off into the wilderness had a scarlet thread tied around its horns. *Though your sins are like scarlet, they shall be as white as snow; though they are red as crimson, they shall be like wool...*' She looked beyond his shoulder into the distance as she quoted Isaiah. 'It's the symbol of sin.'

'Still cool, like I said. What? You looked pissed.'

'No, it's just. I don't know. Odd. You, wearing the symbol of a Christian cult.'

'And that offends you more than this, and this?' He pointed out just one of his many blasphemous tattoos, an image of Baphomet inside a pentagram on the side of his neck.

'Somehow, yes. Just ignore me. Sorry.' They began to walk on, but she couldn't quite let the thought go that it was an odd thing for Jared to give Mikko. Suddenly they heard a voice behind them shout 'Er, excuse me...' and they turned to see a figure marching towards them, preceded by a chocolate brown Labrador who jumped up at Mikko wagging its tail. The figure was a middle-aged man dressed in bottle green wellington boots, a waxed hunting jacket and a tweed coat. Unusual clothes for Liverpool, even if this was a patch of countryside on the edge of the city. As he approached them he used his walking stick to hook the Labrador's collar and pull him down from Mikko.

'You do realise you are trespassing? This is actually private property.'

'Really? I thought it was National Trust?' said Helen, feigning innocence, as she knew full well she wasn't supposed to be there. They had deliberately left the marked path.

'It is, but you still have to apply for a tour. Imagine if we allowed anyone to wander in? The place would be littered with beer cans.'

'True. Sorry, man,' said Mikko. 'And it's a pretty magical place, isn't it?'

'Indeed, it is.' He looked at them up and down, as if considering what to do with them. 'You'll find your way back to the road that way.' He pointed his stick in the direction of the village where they had parked, and stood watching until they were out of sight.

'You're right,' said Helen as they reached the car and looked back towards the forest. 'It is a magical place. I may not be Catholic, but I can understand why the recusants didn't want the magic to disappear.'

'So maybe it didn't disappear,' he said. 'What if it just went into hiding?'

Chapter Twenty

The Heretics had begun as a podcast, graduated to an internet television show, and was now filmed at the Fortune Theatre with a live ticketed audience. The rumour was that Absalom had been courted by several TV networks and commercial sponsors, but had rejected them all, preferring to remain independent. Everyone knew that; how they knew it, no-one was sure.

Tonight's theme was quirky and relatively light-hearted. Entitled 'Are We Alone?' it promised an evening of aliens, UFOs and the truth about progress. It sounded like something from a cheap sci-fi cable channel, or even a parody, although having watched The Heretics debate more weighty controversies like abortion and terrorism, Darren knew by now that it was Absalom's *modus operandi* to draw the trite from the intellectual, the genius from the lunatic. At least somebody would be exposed as a fraud, or a bigot, or a simpleton, but it was often not the person you might expect.

With a backdrop screen that had The Heretics logo, Absalom had set up the stage with four very different chairs. It was designed to look like one of those free-thinking hipster Silicon Valley offices, with furniture of different colours and textures, a sort of soft play area for intellectuals. The lights went down and a hush fell over the crowd. Darren saw figures moving into position, then The Heretics jingle, an ironically pedantic take on the serious news format, was played over the speakers and the lights went up.

Absalom introduced the guests. He spoke a lot. There was a man who believed in ancient astronauts, the pseudoscientific theory that extra-terrestrial beings had visited the earth in ancient times and influenced human culture and development. He was a sweet-looking old Hungarian man, an aristocrat who had devoted his life to his research; a modern-day Phileas Fogg, travelling the world to debunk the human origins of various cultural marvels. 'I also believe that these aliens – these Gods – will come back,' he said, delighted about this belief. 'They left markers to guide their way back. Have we done what they asked?'

Absalom radiated earnest attempts to understand. His manner was far less professional than Amber Rees, but that was its charm. He struggled for the right word, always found it, then followed it with several synonyms, as if there was a thesaurus in his head. He allowed even the stupidest or most abhorrent views to have their say, letting the speaker's words hang. Often nothing else was needed. Cleverer or more nuanced arguments he would take down with faux-naive flair. He combined the beginner's mind attitude with razor-sharp insight. A lot of the charm came from the accent; the Liverpool accent that had always been so unfortunately associated with unsophistication was now liberated and ran free through literary fields of expression, Absalom accentuating certain words with abandon. Darren knew, having watched several shows online, that the camera would pan to Absalom's amused expression just at the right moment, or linger on a struggling guest just a moment too long, to create the perfect dramatic tension. He was like a spider, casting out gossamer threads with which to ensure his victims could not escape. 'We've seen your science, now tell us more about the Biblical origins of your theories.'

The old man beamed. 'The stories of the Nephilim in the Book of Genesis, and the 'Watchers' in the Book of Enoch – these are historical accounts of extra-terrestrials visiting earth. And the Book of Ezekiel clearly refers to spaceships.'

Absalom gave him the floor, uninterrupted, for several minutes, and then gave an earnest analysis, bringing out some of the psychological interest.

'People like to hear about this because of the, the, the profound whimsy of it, but I think it taps into something much deeper within our psyche. This idea about the aliens, the gods, coming back, or being already back, I think all of us, religious or not, have internalised this idea of the Second Coming. That someone is coming to save us from ourselves. That we're not alone. Perhaps it's a comfort.'

Darren shrank down in his seat slightly. He dreaded the thought of Andrew Shepherd being on this show, and his ideas being given credence for the purposes of entertainment.

The ancient astronaut man was countered by a cultural anthropologist who proved beyond any reasonable scientific doubt that the pyramids and Easter Island statues were indeed constructed by humans. She then proceeded to accuse the Hungarian of an inherent racism, in his inability to accept that primitive, non-Western civilisations had the skills and ingenuity to create such things. Darren couldn't really argue with that.

Neither did Absalom, but he had an interesting spin on it. 'You see, what fascinates me most, if I may,' he said, pacing the stage, deep in thought, 'is that I think you know all this. And I even wonder if you know that we know that you know. You don't believe in ancient astronauts any more than myself or our good anthropologist friend here. And yet you choose to believe. You choose to perpetuate the myth. Not because it brings you notoriety, or fortune – even though it does. But because it's just *what you do*.' He accentuated these last three words. 'You believe something, knowing it to be false, so that it becomes itself, conjures itself into being.'

The debate moved on to UFOs. One woman, a former CIA

agent turned whistleblower, was convinced of a long-term international conspiracy to disguise the presence of UFOs. Her valiant battle against an astronomer led Absalom to his conclusion for the evening.

'We've all become obsessed with the idea of being watched. And it's no surprise that this obsession has coincided with the decline of religious belief. Eye in the Sky, Big Brother, revenge porn, stealth advertising… we fear being watched. And yet we want it, we need it. How else can we explain the rise of social media? It's *not* being watched that's our greatest fear. Because if we are not being watched – by UFOs, by gods, by our social media mutuals – these lacerated, meaningless bonds – then we are alone in the universe. And maybe that's our greatest fear. So, what happens if you liberate yourself from the idea that someone is watching? No-one is watching. No-one cares. See you in two weeks.'

It was impossible for him to lose. Either the warring sides found common ground and surprised everyone, or they fought like dogs, exposing each other's moral frailties to the delight and expectation of the audience. It was almost lazy, and certainly irresponsible, but hugely entertaining. Darren felt like a voyeur, but at the same time intensely part of it. He stayed in his seat until the applause petered out, and then dawdled his way out of the seating row and up the stairs, knowing full well he was pretending to text Thomas, and not wanting to hope that Absalom noticed him. James had not met his gaze once during the show, but somehow Darren knew that he would approach him afterwards. There was a certain inevitability to it, but he decided to walk very slowly just in case.

'Darren! You made it. Come to the after-party back at HQ. You'll be my guest.'

He was supposed to be meeting Colette at the pub in half an

hour, it was their usual night. But he decided he could be a bit late. She was always late, she wouldn't mind. 'Ok, just for one then.'

'Fantastic. You head over and I'll meet you when I've finished up here.'

Darren stood awkwardly at the edge of the Liverpool Natural Philosophy Society's main room, half-way between the bar and the library. James had not yet made his entrance, so with time to himself, he scanned the room with his policeman's eye, taking in the surroundings. There were fewer people than he expected, but it was a Wednesday night after all. That pretty girl, Nicole, was serving drinks to the evening's speakers, plus a smattering of people he didn't recognise.

Behind its huge glass front was the Society's magnificent library. At once ancient and modern, ordered and erratic, it was one of those magical libraries with floor to ceiling shelves and fragile spiral staircases, one of which even had a tiny desk perched up at ceiling level. Here and there was a pile of unshelved books, just in case things appeared too neat. There were leather-bound collections of journals, ancient volumes that may never be read again, brand-new copies of the latest academic books, popular science and philosophy.

Darren was intrigued by a section at the back that had a further wall of plexiglass around it, with a locked door marked 'Private.' Inside were ancient-looking leather volumes, some very worn, some enclosed in individual glass cases. The lights were lower in there, and there was specialised equipment for monitoring temperature and humidity.

James arrived and the energy in the room instantly increased. He worked his way through, shaking hands, laughing, pointing, always placing his spare hand on the recipient's arm. It was a cliché but he really did light up the room, Darren thought. It was as if the dimmer switch had been dialled back up to full.

Although they hadn't made eye contact, Darren somehow knew that James' journey through the room was entirely focused on him as the destination, and sure enough he arrived at Darren and handed him a whisky. It wasn't really Darren's drink of choice, but he didn't like to say.

'Very impressive, this library,' he said, motioning behind him. 'What's that all about?'

'Oh, the sealed off area? That is William Merchant's private collection from the seventeenth century. Or what's left of it, anyway. Some of them date back to antiquity. The British Library and the Bodleian have been trying to get their hands on that collection for decades.'

'But you'll never sell?'

'Not only will we never sell, we won't even let them look. They don't even know what they are missing. That's the beauty of it.'

'What are they missing?'

'Perhaps nothing. Perhaps everything. Just because something is ancient doesn't mean it is valuable – there was just as much drivel written two thousand years ago as there is today. Actually, that's not true at all. But you get my point. Or perhaps we have some crucial text in there that will solve mysteries, secrets hidden since the foundation of the world. I love to infuriate people.'

'I noticed - tonight on the stage.'

'You'll have access to the texts in there if you become a member. If I don't infuriate you so much that you give up.'

'Oh, I don't think there will be anything for me.'

'You'd be surprised.'

This speaking in riddles felt almost like flirtation, and Darren realised that James was standing close to him, slightly invading his personal space. Perhaps he did this with everyone, in order to intimidate them. Yes, that's what Darren told himself. As he felt his heartbeat quicken slightly.

'Can I show you something?' James said, apparently on a whim.
'Sure.'

Darren followed him into the library and started towards the private area, but James kept moving towards the very back.

'Oh, I thought you were going to show me...'

'The secret books? Oh no, not until you reach membership status. No this is something else!'

At the back of the library they began climbing a rickety spiral iron staircase, and at the top James unscrewed a circular hatch. As if they were going up through a manhole.

'Come on then!' Darren followed him and they emerged onto the roof of Horrox house.

The city was ranged out before them. The evening sounds of traffic, sirens, voices, music from neighbouring clubs and bars, and industrial air vents and chimneys, all blended together into a comforting white noise, punctuated by the odd siren, aeroplane, a fog horn, a singular raucous laugh.

And the sky. It was a glorious night. There had been a strong wind all day, and it had chased away all semblance of cloud. Despite the city lights, the sky was so clear that stars could be made out clearly.

''Magnificent, isn't it?' said James. 'I had a feeling tonight would be a good night. Jeremiah Horrox dreamt of building an observatory here. For him, religion and astronomy were one and the same. He was sure that the stars would lead him to some revelation.'

'Like an epiphany?'

'Yes, but it's more… more concrete than that. Something specific. The supernatural revealing itself in the real world. The breakthrough of the sacred or the supernatural into reality. A… a, a, a… hierophany, if you will.'

'You like big words, don't you?'

'I do. So did Horrox. But he died at only twenty-one, you know. Then the Civil War got in the way, and the observatory never happened. Sometimes I wonder if I could do something in his honour. Set up a radio telescope up here. But of course, how was Horrox to know that light pollution would crush that idea. There can be few worse places to build an observatory than the middle of a metropolis. This is a rare night of celestial splendour.'

'It sounds stupid,' said Darren, wishing he had a vocabulary to compete with James' powers of expression, 'but I always used to be scared of the stars when I was little. I still am, to be honest. They make me feel cold, shivery, you know.'

'Really,' James smiled, "Why? Do you feel like they are watching you?'

'No. It's the opposite, actually. I read in a book once that the light we see from a star is millions of years old. We are looking at something that happened millions of years ago, and that star might already be dead. It seems like the saddest thing in the world.'

'I never had you down as a romantic, Darren.'

'I'm not, sorry. Ignore me.' Darren shuffled, embarrassed. He felt terribly out of his depth. On the edge of a precipice. Literally, as well as metaphorically, because the wind had got up again, and a sudden gust knocked them both unsteady on their feet. James took him by the arm and led him away from the edge.

'It does make you dizzy with incomprehension, certainly. It's almost too much to bear. And yet, when confronted with scales like that, everything that happens down here feels rather insignificant. And that can be comforting too, don't you think?'

'Yes.' Darren had often told himself this. Even though he knew it was a cop-out. The worst sort of cop-out.

They sat back on the ledge of the sloping part of the roof, at a safe distance from the edge.

'I… er… noticed that Andrew Shepherd is on the billing for a podcast debate in June,' he ventured.

'Andrew Shepherd, let me see. Ah, the geneticist? Yes,

absolutely. We've got him on with the evolutionary biologist Marta Reyes. Why do you mention him?'

'How much do you know about him?'

'That he's a rogue geneticist,' James said this with ironic delectation, placing the two words in the air with his hands. 'How cavalier those words are together – such a magnificent oxymoron. Fired from the Human Genome Project, he thinks he's found the gene for sin and that he can send everyone to Heaven. Wonderful.'

Absalom said it with glee, and Darren was irritated. But then of course, he reminded himself, James wasn't to know that he had been the detective on the case. He could only know what he had read in the papers about Shepherd. The sensational stories about what Andrew had yelled in court.

James noticed. 'You look disapproving, Darren.'

'I was the lead detective on Andrew Shepherd's case. What you say is true, but there's a lot more to it than that. Andrew's actions led to a series of murders. The murder of a pregnant teenager, a young lad crucified, a man's foot amputated... I don't think he is someone you want to give the floor to. Apart from anything else, he's mentally ill.'

James looked amused to be challenged. 'By whose definition is he mentally ill? Yours? The state's? What he says is unfalsifiable. That's why I love it. He can't prove it, but you can't disprove it either. It's a new type of science. A post-science, if you will.'

'I'm just not sure it's right to put vulnerable people up there on that platform, and expose them to everyone.'

'But what is vulnerability? I think we could all do with being a little more vulnerable. Again, I apply to Andrew Shepherd the same criteria I apply to everyone. Extraordinary claims require extraordinary evidence. So let him do his thing.'

'It's going to be explosive.'

'Exactly.'

James was practically rubbing his hands together, and Darren decided to let it go, but he was quiet, thinking about Andrew Shepherd. He decided there was no need to press the point. Because the uncomfortable truth was that he wasn't at all sure whether Andrew Shepherd was mentally ill. The possibility lingered like a ghost upon his consciousness that Andrew Shepherd might be right.

Absalom continued, and he was well-informed on the Shepherd case. 'You know he believes he can create the Second Coming? It's fantastic. It's the stuff internet dreams are made of. The trial was legendary – I was absolutely gripped by the news reports.'

Darren wondered whether to tell James that Andrew Shepherd didn't just believe that he could create the Second Coming, he believed that he *had* created the Second Coming. That baby, Elizabeth, had been born to a girl treated with Shepherd's gene therapy, to replace a guanine with adenine at position 32 in her DNA, a single base change in the OS1 gene that Shepherd called the 'marker for Heaven.' And then a virgin conception, achieved through artificial insemination via a needle through the abdomen, the hymen unbroken. Shepherd had no doubt about what had occurred. And Darren sometimes wondered what he himself really thought about it. Because it was ridiculous. Wasn't it?

He felt himself being constantly drawn back to Sandy Lane, that street of mansions in Blundellsands, not so much because Thomas lived there, but because Elizabeth lived there with her foster family. He had bumped into Andrew Shepherd more than once, hanging around. And had not reported him, despite the restraining order. *She needs to be protected. Only you can protect her, Detective.*

Only thoughts of Matt prevented these words from being his last thought before sleep, and his first thought on waking in the morning.

'I can see you're bothered by this. You have strong morals, and I respect that.'

Aware that he was being tested, Darren decided to acquiesce. And perhaps James did have a point. There were so many different ways of looking at the world, and James Absalom seemed to see the world in technicolour. Perhaps he could learn something from that.

Darren's phone buzzed in his pocket again. He had been aware of it vibrating several times during the evening, but he had been enjoying the feeling of being off-grid, of feeling no urge at all to check and see who it was. So engrossed was he in what he was doing, in the person he was with. And then he remembered Colette. A missed call and three text messages.

Are you on your way mate? I feel like a right billy-no-mates sat here on me own...

It's been nearly an hour... I'm going home. Hope everything's ok.

Darren? I'm a bit worried, it's not like you. Call me. I'm at home.

Shit.

Chapter Twenty-One

Darren jumped into a taxi and headed for Colette's place. He could grab a bottle of that white wine she liked from the off-licence on the corner; maybe he could salvage the evening. But on the way, he checked the news on his phone, and the off-licence was almost forgotten, so engrossed was he. Grabbing the first bottle of white wine he saw, he virtually threw the money onto the counter.

'*Wild Woman Found Dead*' read the headline.

The 'Wild Woman of Blundellsands', identified last week as Diane Goodwin, a woman who went missing nearly thirty years ago, was found dead in her hospital room in Aintree General. An inquest will be held, but foul play has been ruled out, and the cause of death is suicide.

There were lights on in Colette's front room, and he could see through the net curtains that she was watching TV on the couch. She put the chain on the door before answering, and when she saw it was Darren she released the chain, but reluctantly. She stood in the half-open doorway, blocking the entrance. He was clearly not invited in. She was in pyjama bottoms, but he could see that she still hadn't taken off her make-up after the evening's disappointment.

'I'm really sorry,' he said, shuffling in the cold air, and he meant it, but knew it wasn't good enough. 'Something came up and....'

'And you couldn't even send me a message?'

'I messed up. Sorry.' He held up the bottle of wine as a peace offering. 'What about if we have that drink now?'

'Darren, it's half past eleven. I've got work in the morning. Another time, eh.' She began to close the door, but he held up the newspaper with his other hand.

'Hey, speaking of work, why didn't you tell me the Wild Woman was dead?'

He was deflated to see that not only was she not excited to talk about it, she was pissed off.

'Because it's not your case! It's nothing to do with you, and I should never have told you about it in the first place. I could lose my job because of you!'

'I'm sorry. But it was you who first brought it up. I thought… I thought I was helping you, just as a mate, you know.'

Colette studied him for a minute, a bitterness in her face that he hadn't seen before. She relinquished her hold on the door and sank a little.

'Are we even mates? Ever since this wild woman thing started all you've been interested in is grilling me for details of the case. You haven't once asked me how I am, whether I've got a new boyfriend...'

'Have you...'

'You don't care! And anyway, when were you planning to tell me about your new boyfriend? How stupid did I feel, turning up to the pub to find Thomas Kuper there like it was nothing? Helen and that Mikko bloke all in-the-know, and you've all got your in-jokes and secrets.'

Darren began to prepare an indignant response, but quickly realised that he deserved everything she said. He was not a good friend, and had taken Colette for granted. What was wrong with him?

As they looked at each other, both a little sad that their friendship had been damaged, they also shared the unspoken knowledge that Diane Goodwin's death was not a simple case of suicide. And now they couldn't even talk about it.

Chapter Twenty-Two

This could theoretically be misconstrued as stalking, Helen thought to herself. Then she admitted to herself that there was no 'theoretical' or 'misconstrued' about it – she was stalking. But with a good reason, she was sure of it.

Having left her car at Blundellsands & Crosby train station, she was walking down Belmont Avenue, as she had done every day this week, at different times of day, trying to tread a line in her demeanour somewhere between furtive and nonchalant. She would slow down her pace as much as she dared, take her walk on the beach and then do the same on the way back, but she hadn't seen a soul all week. Until today.

Just after she had passed the monastery, she heard the front door close, and then footsteps. She glanced back and there he was, rounding the gate and coming towards her, the skirt of his brown robe swishing around his feet that incongruously wore Nike trainers. He wore the same anorak he had been wearing when she saw in the garden that day.

Helen fumbled with her phone on the corner, pretending to be occupied until he caught up with her.

'Excuse me, Owen?'

He had his hands clasped in front of him, head bowed, but then he jumped. She had startled him.

'Sorry. I didn't mean to... sorry. I'm Helen. I came to visit the monastery a few weeks ago and I saw you in the garden.'

Owen looked benignly expectant, nodded and smiled vaguely. He had a weary face, a face that had lived beyond its years. He looked apologetic, and made signs to show that he couldn't speak.

'Of course, your vows of silence. But you can listen, if you like, as we walk.'

She motioned towards the beach. Owen seemed anxious now, and looked from the monastery to the beach as if deciding how to make his escape from this woman.

'I used to be a nun, you know,' she continued. 'And there aren't many young people who take the vows these days, so I just thought you might like to chat. You know, before...'

He hesitated, then began walking fast towards the beach, holding up his hands in apology. Helen made after him, so he quickened his pace into a stride, his skirt flapping, and she had to scamper to keep up.

'Owen. Please.'

Eventually he stopped, but only stared straight ahead, as if to show he would only barely tolerate what she had to say.

'Listen, Owen. I've been exactly where you are. Well, almost exactly.'

Now he looked at her, inquiring.

'I took religious vows. I became a nun – out of some misplaced sense of guilt. I thought I was atoning for something I did, but I was wrong. I made a terrible mistake and wasted ten years of my life.'

Owen was shaking his head now and, sighing, he turned around and began to walk back towards the monastery. But Helen turned around too *like a terrier, I was*, she thought afterwards, *snapping at his heels*. She noticed that her voice was becoming shriller, imploring.

'I think you're about to make an even worse mistake than me. I escaped, but you might not be so lucky.' She wondered if she should say more, tell him about the skeletons, about her theory. She felt she knew this young man intimately, this boy with the tattooed neck and earrings and acne scars, who still looked older than his years, as old as the world itself, betrayed by the sadness in his eyes. She knew that sadness. Felt it every time she closed her own eyes and saw the limp body of her little brother hanging from the blinds, heard her own screams. Perhaps Owen too had been responsible for someone's death. Her mother had said it was the most monstrous egotism to become a nun, to make it all about her. And while nothing she did would ever have earned her mother's forgiveness, in a sense her mother had been right. The only way to atone is to forgive yourself and try to live a good life.

They were back at the gate of the monastery now. Owen looked up nervously and Helen followed his eyes to an upstairs window from which Father Angelo and another monk were watching them. Owen shrugged sadly and went inside.

She walked back towards her car, feeling dejected and guilty. She had misjudged that so badly. Perhaps she was losing her touch. So wrapped up in her own perspective, that all she had achieved was depriving him of his daily walk. And yet. And yet. If she could prevent him from becoming the next Diane...

Chapter Twenty-Three

Darren woke between crisp, Egyptian cotton sheets, to the scent of fresh linen, Thomas' aftershave and scented candles. In the quarter-light of dawn he took in his surroundings; Thomas's lean, muscular back next to him, a plush-carpeted room that was far too large for a bedroom, an oversized flatscreen TV mounted on the wall opposite, with a sofa area on which their clothes from last night were strewn. When he woke up at home in Waterloo, less than two miles away, he would hear the rumble of traffic along Liverpool Road, the clanking of machinery at the docks, and the squawking of seagulls. Here there was silence, not a car in the street at this hour, far from any traffic. And just when he was thinking how quiet it was, there came a piercing shriek, muffled by distance since they were at the front of the house, but distinctly a bird. It was that bloody peacock in Thomas' back garden.

Darren had childishly hoped that the peacock would miraculously disappear like Justine had, but it was still there, stalking him, judging him, creeping him out. And Thomas said it reminded him of home, his village in Switzerland. The thought of Thomas' home creeped Darren out too. He knew sleep would not return now, so he rolled on to his back to contemplate the day ahead, to contemplate everything.

He and Thomas went way back; before Matt, before Darren had become a detective. He had been doing security on the house during matches, when footballers were vulnerable to burglary since the whole world knew they were out. Then he had switched to close protection when there had been a series of threats against the team's stars. Nothing had ever happened back then, but he and Thomas had awakened something in each other. Their eyes would meet, in the rear-view mirror or across the bonnet of a car, through the garden window. And somehow ,Darren knew that the series of glamorous girlfriends meant nothing, and somehow Thomas knew that Darren was more than just another uniform. They spoke little, but their words to each other meant everything.

It was only years later, when Thomas was married to Justine Killy and Darren engaged to Matt, that Darren discovered just how much he and Thomas had in common. They had both been brought up in the clutches of religious cults. Darren's parents were members of the controversial Mainstreet Church, and as a teenager he had been forced to undergo conversion therapy and told every day that his very identity amounted to a demonic possession. Thomas had grown up in a remote Swiss village where arcane Catholic rituals were combined with a dark occultism, where the inhabitants appeared to view demonic possession as a good thing. Darren had abandoned his childhood and turned his back on religion. Had Thomas? Was he a little scared of Thomas?

Darren had never told him that during the investigation into the deaths of Eliza Bektashi and the Dock Road Eight, he and Helen had visited the village and met Thomas' sinister grandmother. How could they not have talked about that?

'It's going to come back to bite you one day,' Helen had warned him, and somehow he didn't worry about it. It was all part of his low-level turmoil, only one more of the many secrets he kept. But it was ridiculous to have a relationship built on so many layers of secrets. And that thought, pathetically, made him feel better about the possibility of its demise.

Suddenly Darren became aware of an unnerving presence in the room, and was startled into a sitting position by the sight of Alfie in the doorway.

'Dada?'

Darren had always thought of himself as someone who liked kids, but this kid, who had the potential to become his stepson, freaked him out. In the little boy's eyes, Darren saw Justine, and Shawn Forrest, not simply because they were his biological parents, but because it was as if they were still here. It was as if Alfie knew. And Darren hated himself for taking out his paranoias on a toddler.

'Hello mate,' he said. 'Wake up early then?'

Alfie held on to the door uncertainly, and Darren shook Thomas awake. 'Hey, Alfie's here.'

Thomas rolled out of bed and sleepily began attending to Alfie in French, ushering him out of the room.

Darren sat up straight in bed and then emerged to retrieve his phone from the low table in front of the TV. Next to the phone on the table was Thomas' invitation to the Northern Sports Awards that evening, where he was to be honoured with an award. Darren imagined them going together, hand in hand, smiling for photographers. And couldn't imagine it.

In these academic days there was rarely anything waiting for him on his phone screen in the morning, but today he saw a 6.30am message from Helen.

'I hope Thomas is ok. If you're over there, check the coast is clear outside before leaving.'

He had no idea what it meant, but there were some noises coming from the front of the house. Darren leapt up and went to the window where he parted the curtain very slightly. The front garden was protected from the road by a high hedge, but through the gaps in the electric gates he could see there were several vans parked outside, and he could hear a faint clamour of voices. And on the other side of the road, two separate photographers were fiddling with their equipment, and a TV camera crew was setting up. Darren quickly closed the curtains, and searched the news on his phone. He didn't have to search hard. There was a stream of headlines '*Super Kuper requests transfer... Betrayal... Kuper's Gay Lover...*'

It was happening. 'Thomas,' he called. 'You need to get in here.'

Alfie hooked into one elbow, Thomas peered over Darren's shoulder at the crowd outside. His face was ashen.

'You always knew this was a possibility,' Darren said. 'The transfer. The gay thing. It's all come at once. Maybe it's a good thing?'

Thomas put Alfie down and paced around the room, hands to his mouth, hands behind his head. Then he sat on the sofa with his head in his hands.

'Dada?'

Alfie tried to climb on him. 'Here mate, I'll put a cartoon on, shall I?' Darren grabbed the remote and switched on some frantic animation, and over its din he sat next to Thomas to console him.

'What if we just walk out there together this morning? We don't say anything, and you just drive to training as usual? Like it's not even a thing? Footballers are allowed to get transfers. Footballers are allowed to be gay.'

'Come on, Darren.'

'Let me go out there with you. Or if not this morning, then tonight?' He wafted the invitation at Thomas. 'We could go together.'

'No, not here. But you could come with me abroad. We can start again, somewhere else. I just don't want to deal with it. I gave them nine years. Why can't they leave me alone?'

'I know it's not fair. You pay a heavy price for all this. But we can do something good, think about it. And if you can't be yourself here, you can't be yourself anywhere. People love you in Liverpool, and they're the most tolerant people in the world. I'm sorry, but I've been through too much to go back into hiding. I don't want to live like that anymore.'

'Neither do I.'

'Anyway, what would I do in fucking Madrid or wherever?'

'I hear the weather is good...' Thomas smiled weakly.

'Ok, so what if I just walk out the front door?'

'Darren, you can't.'

'I know I can't. When will I be able to? When?'

Thomas stared at the table. 'I don't know.'

'Fine. I'll sneak out the back. Just think about tonight, ok?'

Darren was on edge all day. He checked his phone every five minutes to see if Thomas had called or messaged. He tried to imagine how James Absalom would handle a situation like this, and felt suddenly energized by the thought of the effortless wit and breezy confidence he would employ. For the first time in his life he felt like blazing a trail, making a difference, being a cause. But he heard nothing from Thomas, and on the local six o'clock news that evening, a smiling Thomas was hand-in-hand with a local glamour girl who had been arranged for him, the two of them blinking in the glare of flashlights. Surely it was over between them now, and he would have to find the strength to end it officially. But there was still the hope and fear that he wouldn't. Maybe Thomas' agent had arranged the girl, maybe he had given him no choice, maybe there was still something to salvage.

When Darren's phone lit up, he hoped it would be a quick apology from Thomas. Maybe he was regretting taking that girl to the awards, maybe he was thinking of him right at this moment. *Please let him be thinking of me.* It was an odd feeling – as if he didn't exist. That he was utterly surplus to this world, and not a single person knew.

The message was not from Thomas but from James, with characteristically erudite, flamboyant text. And Darren found he was not disappointed. Someone who valued his company.

Man hath no better thing under the sun, than to eat, and to drink, and

*to be merry. And so, I command the enjoyment of life. And I command
you to have dinner with me tonight. What say you?*

It was serendipity, in fact. Was that the definition of serendipity?
Perfect timing?

On Saturday night an impromptu restaurant table in the city
centre should have been an impossibility, but James had secured
them a table at Brown's, the latest place to be seen, only a few
steps from the five-star hotel where right now Thomas would be
presenting at the glittering awards ceremony.

When Darren arrived, weaving his way past packed dinner
tables and adjusting his ears to the chatter and music, James was
already waiting, glued to his phone. Darren went to shake his
hand but James moved in for a hug. They sat down and surveyed
together, in friendly conspiracy, the tables around them.

'Well, this feels a bit like a date, doesn't it?' grinned James, eyes
shining. 'In fact, are you married? I never asked.'

'I was engaged. But… he died.'

'I'm so sorry. Do you mind if I ask how he died?'

'He was a firefighter. He died in the Pinnacle explosion.'

'My god. I'm so sorry. So, he died a martyr's death.'

'I'm not sure he would have said that. But he loved his job.'

'And nobody new?'

'No, not really.' *Why am I lying, why am I lying?*

'So, Darren, you've attended three of our events now. What do
you think?'

Every event Darren attended seemed to speak directly to him,
yet challenge him, yet validate him. He felt himself growing. He
felt at home. More than he had in the police, more than he did
at university, and certainly more far more than he did in Thomas'
world of football and glamour and shame.

'To say they are refreshing would be an understatement. It's
bold, what you do. It feels like… everything and nothing at the

same time. Sorry, that doesn't make any sense.'

'It makes perfect sense. I couldn't have put it better – in fact I feel like writing that down. I shall shamelessly plagiarise you like I do everyone else. It's bold because we are not afraid to speak outside the Overton window.'

'Overton window?'

'The acceptable window of discussion. The range of views deemed palatable to the majority. Anything outside of that is vulnerable to this cancel culture that everyone is afraid of. But no-one can cancel me.'

'Some people would say you're falsely equating viewpoints that are not equal at all. Morally speaking.'

'According to whom?' James leaned forward, excited to explain. 'You see, I prefer to respect my audience. They are smart enough to make up their own minds. I don't punch down, you see. Take that ancient astronaut guy. He was fragile, so there was no need for me to go all out. Obviously, he's an old-school racist, but I let the audience figure that out for themselves. Of course, he was ill-equipped to battle the anthropologist. But I believe that people motivated by malice or immorality will reveal themselves. Like a modern-day Count of Monte Cristo, I'm simply facilitating the means of others' self-destruction.' He smiled and leaned back. 'What are you thinking?'

'I'm thinking you like words a lot.'

'And you don't. You're very laconic, Darren, and that makes a nice change. It's mysterious. I know people think my show is vulgar. But the thing is, vulgarity is inherently subversive. I loathe the unctuous sanctimony that can descend on liberal politics, these paroxysms of wokeness that stifle real debate. Aggressive disaffection, neoliberal incrementalism.' He wafted his hands around, searching for phrases. 'I like to be the ringmaster, using derision as a weapon of mass destruction. Against the innate savagery of our species.'

Darren couldn't argue with that, as a murder detective who

had seen plenty of the innate savagery of which humans were capable.

'Anyway, tell me about your family, Darren. Have they supported you through what must have been a very difficult time? Liverpool is a place of such close families.'

Darren smiled grimly and shook his head. 'I'm… what do you call it… estranged from my family. It's complicated. Actually, it's not complicated. My parents are members of the Mainstreet Church.' Darren looked at James to see his reaction, and he raised his eyebrows appropriately.

'A veritable cult. So that was your childhood. I can't imagine your coming out went well, then.'

'They have a programme for that. Conversion therapy.'

They both raised their eyebrows and drank silently.

'What about your parents then?' Darren asked.

'No matter what I did I was a perennial disappointment to my father. For my twenty-first birthday he gave me a copy of Turgenev's "Diary of A Superfluous Man." Do you know it?'

Darren shook his head.

'In the 1840s and 1850s the Russians had a literary concept of the "failson".' He made a theatrical motion of inverted commas with his fingers. 'Failson, what a damning term. Although I must admit I rather liked the Byronic romance of it. A failson is the epitome of the superfluous man, born into privilege, talented and intelligent, but with no integrity or ambition. Typical behaviours are gambling, drinking, romantic intrigues and duels. I haven't tried a duel – yet.' Darren laughed.

'Doomed to live out my life in passivity, that's me.'

'But he would have been proud of you now, surely.'

'He would have loathed what I'm doing now.'

'Really? Because it's attention-seeking?'

'No.' James looked slightly put out at this, and Darren regretted it. *Why can't I ever say anything nice?* 'No, because of the vulgarity of it. Because I'm a hobbyist, because what I do has no concrete, no substance to it. Utter froth – I can just hear him. But here's the thing. In the Natural Philosophy Society, and on The Heretics, we will discuss the tritest cultural event with depth and integrity. Because what I do is this: the revealing of truths. Things hidden from the world. Truths people have hidden from themselves. Because I think they should know. We care about the things no-one else cares about. The perceived humiliations. The mass of vulnerabilities. The different languages for what the truth means. Anyway, whatever. As they say. All of this,' he swatted at imaginary flies around him, 'this, this, this… life… it all amounts to the mere convulsions of a dying star. Humanity is at the disposal of blind forces.'

Ordinarily Darren would have stopped listening half-way through a speech like that, but tonight the poetic nihilism fed into his current state of mind.

'So, I suppose part of what I'm doing is an enormous 'fuck you' to my father – to find the most publicly idiotic and vacuous thing I could possibly do. Worse than doing nothing in private, I am doing worse than nothing in public. But there's also the vain hope that somehow, I might actually make a difference. And that would be the biggest fuck you of all. After all, the twenty-first century is basically defined by non-essential human beings, who do not fit into the market as consumers or producers or as labourers. So perhaps I am the epitome of the twenty-first century man. Well, the authority of the father and the revolt of the son – a perennial human tale. So perhaps I represent both history and modernity. Let's drink to that.'

Darren worried that he was also about to become a superfluous man. God, could there be anything worse.

'Do you not worry that one day you'll be taken down?'

'No, because there is no mask to unmask. What you see is what you get. And as for my political views, they sway in the wind. I am inviolable to that knee-jerk self-righteousness. Radical honesty – from the guests – it's the only way to authenticity.'

'Except – you are sort of alienated.'

'Am I though? And more than anyone else? We're all islands these days. And what I do is in permanent air quotes, the inauthenticity is the appeal. It's the post-ironic mystique that I cultivate. I know, and you know that I know. You know you're being satirised, and you allow it. Post-meaning. It's art. Well, shall we order?'

Chapter Twenty-Four

Darren was running past Hawthorne Park, feeling the pulse of blood through his ears. His sense of unease was all the more disturbing because he couldn't quite define its cause. He and Thomas were no longer together, but there had been no closure. Because there had been nothing official to start with. It had remained almost as ephemeral than it had been years before. He had no idea whether or not he had made a terrible mistake. Maybe he should have taken a risk, taken Thomas at his word, and gone with him. Some instinct, however, told him to stay here; not because he loved the place, but because he had some undefined duty to fulfil, and it had something to do with that baby Elizabeth. And some instinct gave him a sense of relief that Thomas was leaving, and in particular that Alfie was leaving.

Darren was also uneasy because he feared that he had created a story out of nothing. If you go looking for clues, patterns, you will find them. And his brain was a trained pattern-seeking engine that was now freed from the shackles of police procedure. It could simply be a homeless woman and a collection of bones. His own mantra – there are no coincidences – he was afraid to apply here. In these strange days of speculation, nothing felt quite real, as if it didn't really matter if he was wrong.

As Darren rounded the corner of Warren Road, he heard the sounds of building work coming from within Hawthorne Park, and then he saw between the trees the roof and shovel of a JCB earth mover. The dull roar of machinery and intermittent shouts of men, the background din of a radio. He had checked the planning records for this area - there were no public works. There had been two applications for house extensions on Warren Road, but nothing like this.

But of course, Hawthorne Park was owned by a private foundation. They didn't need to make a public application. He cursed himself for not having thought of this. And now he needed to get in. He jogged up and down the pavement for a few moments on his tiptoes, neck craned, trying to catch the attention of one of the builders. He even shouted *Hey, mate!* but it was futile - they were too far away. With the spiked railings, green-painted, in front of him, he contemplated trying to climb over, realised it was absurd. At the same moment, he knew that the wild woman's gash came from these railings. She had been in here, he was sure of it now. He then contemplated sneaking into the park through the adjacent tennis club, as he had done when he was a teenager, and realised he was indeed going to do it.

He doubled-back to the tennis club, running as nonchalantly as he could through the car park. There was a group of older women playing doubles, and he kept his gaze ahead, mildly amused at his childish fear of being caught. If he remembered correctly, there was a place behind the bins where the fence was wire only, with no metal spikes, and he could vault over. Ungracefully, he did so, repeating a move he had made almost twenty years before, and he was in. He now had to backtrack through the park, all around the perimeter of the tennis courts, in order to reach the building site.

'Hey mate, what are you building here?' He spoke to a man in dirty high-vis jacket and hard hat, putting his hands on his hips to catch his breath, trying to sound only mildly interested.

'New bowling club, apparently.' You'd have to ask the boss though, we're just clearing the area.'

Daren looked around – there were felled trees, piles of uprooted bushes, and ground-levelling equipment. This had been a tiny piece of wilderness.

'What's that over there?'

He had seen a cylindrical iron cover, like a manhole cover, except raised off the ground. It looked old, possibly very old, and was surrounded by vegetation.

'To be honest, I don't know,' said the builder. 'We haven't got there yet. Are you a member of the park committee or something?'

'Excuse me mate, this is a restricted area.' A foreman was approaching.

'Why?'

'Why? Because it's a building site. We don't know what's down there yet. We're waiting for a civil engineer before we go in.'

Darren wanted to say 'I have reason to believe it's connected to a police inquiry.' But he couldn't. And he didn't even have enough evidence to ask Colette to get a warrant. And then, if they had been on speaking terms.

He contemplated coming back at the crack of dawn to explore the place alone, but decided to take a leaf out of Helen's book and improvise. Who knew who else was involved? There was no time to lose.

'I am a civil engineer actually, so if you want I can take a look. Just informally, you know. Looks like a simple storm drain to me.'

The foreman thought for a moment. 'Go-ed then! The more time we save on this the better. Here – you need a hard hat.'

Together Darren and the foreman levered off the heavy metal disc. And then looked at each other, eyes wide. It looked like there was a room down there, and there was still a faint smell of human waste, as if this place had been lived in recently. One after the other they lowered themselves down the metal ladder rungs, and made the drop into a small room. It was like a war bunker, perhaps *was* a war bunker. The walls were lined with concrete and bricks, and the ceiling with steel. There was a ventilation system, a water supply, a separate area with a primitive toilet, and even an electric light bulb, with power lines rewired from the local grid. It was liveable – just. But for thirty years? The place had clearly been swept – there was nothing there. Except for a coffin-shaped hole in the floor. *Look upon your open grave*, he remembered from The Ancrene Riwle. And except for the walls, which were lined with carvings and scrawlings. Darren had no time to examine them because a voice called down to them from the shaft, followed by the uniformed figure of the warden who appeared on the ladder and peered in. He looked familiar, and Darren thought he might be the same warden that had thrown his teenage self out of the park all those years ago.

'Excuse me. Can I see your membership card? What's going on here?'

'I could ask you the same question: this is a police investigation.'

He was effectively impersonating a police officer, which he knew better than anyone was a fairly significant crime, but he needed to be down there. Once the real police arrived, he would lose his chance. The warden lowered himself down too, making the drop gingerly, and Darren was careful to notice his reaction. If he knew about this place, he was a very good actor. He looked stunned.

Darren called Colette. 'Colette. It's about the Wild Woman case. You need to get down to Hawthorne Park with a team. Warren Road entrance.'

'Darren,' she sighed, 'I asked you to stay off this case. Please. It's too much.'

'No, listen. Colette. I've found it. I've found where Diane was being kept.'

Darren stood behind the police line. It was midday now, and he was still in his running gear. He should have gone home to shower and change hours ago, but he hadn't wanted to leave the place, in case it disappeared. As if he had dreamed it, and if he stopped looking at it, it might stop being real. It was a cool day and his sweat had congealed on his skin and seeped into his bones.

Colette vaulted over the line and came over. 'You were right. I hate to say it. They're fingerprinting the place now, but I think it's been swept. I don't think we'll get any physical evidence.'

'Yeah, it looks as if someone has cleared it out. Those bones could easily have been in the grave area.'

'I've got something to show you.' She held up her iPad, to show him a screenshot of Diane Goodwin's card.

'*Vade in Pacem*,' he read. 'Doesn't that mean go in peace? What is it?'

'This is the card that Diane Goodwin received with her flowers in the hospital. I saw it written on the walls down there as well. It must have meant something to her, something more than just 'go in peace.'

Darren made a mental note to ask Helen later.

'Right,' said Colette, 'we'll take the park warden in for questioning. Jeff Wheeler. He's been here forever apparently. There's going to be absolute uproar when this gets out.'

'You'll need a list of everyone who has a key to this park.'

'What if it's not a keyholder? I used to sneak in here when I was a kid.'

'The warden is fastidious. He hardly ever lets anyone get away. Nothing gets past him.'

'Someone could have copied, stolen a key.'

'No, you can't copy these keys.'

'Between the fancy keys, the spiked railings, and the eagle-eyed tennis players, this park is like Fort Knox.'

'And people are so grateful to be part of the club, why would they question a closed-off area that doesn't bother anyone? It just looks like a patch of unkempt wilderness.

'Who are they?' Darren pointed to a man and a woman, both in business suits having been called from work, poring over a map.

'The Chairman of the tennis club, and Hawthorne Park's equivalent. According to the park map, it is part of the tennis club. According to the tennis club deeds, it's part of the park.

Lamb of God

Nobody ever questioned it until recently when the bowling club proposal was mooted, and the respective committees realised they could do an amicable deal to redevelop it. '

A tiny piece of nowhere, right in the middle of everything.
Someone must have a key for that...

Chapter Twenty-Five

Jeff Wheeler sat in interview room one, looking terrified as the duty solicitor explained what was about to happen. Colette and McGregor watched through the mirrored window.

'He looks like a nervous wreck, doesn't he?'

'He's about to go down for kidnapping, false imprisonment, and incitement to suicide, so... yeah. He would be terrified. Come on, let's go in.'

'Mr. Wheeler, how long have you been working as the warden of Hawthorne Park?'

'Twenty-two years.'

'And what does the job entail?'

'Gardening and security.'

'You do all the gardening yourself?'

'Mostly, yes. It's wilded, so there's not that much. If there's a big job that needs doing, I arrange a contractor. But it's mainly maintenance. And I patrol the park twice a day.'

'You patrol the park twice a day. But not the whole park. Tell us about the manhole cover at the building site.'

'But that area, you see, it's not part of my remit.'

'It's right in the middle of the park.'

'But it's not part of my remit, that's what I'm telling you. I was always told that area was owned by the tennis club and was not to be touched.'

'It's funny, because the tennis club says different. They say that although they own the land, it was supposed to be under the care of the park trust.'

'Then, there must have been some miscommunication. I mean, you can see, the area hasn't been tended in the same way. It's overgrown, unkempt.'

'But you said the park was wilded.'

'Yes, but not like that. It used to annoy me, I had to put it out of my head. I would have gone in to tidy up a bit, but I didn't even have access, there was a fence around it until the building works began. The gate in the fence had its own key. I often wondered who had a key for that, but I never… like I said… I was told it didn't belong to us.'

'So, you're saying you never set foot in that area before?'

'That's what I'm telling you. I've never set foot inside that area. I was as shocked as you to discover that…'

'To discover what?'

'That… there was someone living down there. That's what people are saying, isn't it? That woman was living down there. The Wild Woman who died.'

The man looked genuinely heartbroken. 'I don't know how this could have happened, on my watch.'

'Mr Wheeler, we still don't know exactly what happened down there. But someone had access. Someone was going in there to provide her with food at the very least. Perhaps spending time down there.'

'There're no CCTV anywhere in the park?'

'Only at the tennis club entrance. The place is supposed to be a haven, free from observation. Like a black spot or whatever you call it. Policing it is my job.'

'And from what I've heard, you do it very well. There's about one thousand key holders on this list. Would you recognise a name?'

'I'm sure I would, yes.'

'Does the name Tony Norris mean anything to you?'

He looked blank.

'No. He's not on the list.'

Colette held the list in front of her.

'What about…' Colette hesitated for a moment, and thought of the monastery, just around the corner from Hawthorne Park, and their links with Keystone House.

She scanned the list. And there it was. Father Angelo Zotti.

'What about Angelo Zotti?'

'The monk? Yes… the monks have a key. They share it. We don't normally allow sharing, but they've just always had one.'

'Do you remember anything strange about the first week of March? Anything unusual happen? Any people you don't normally see? Anyone acting strangely?'

He shook his head.

Colette remembered Darren's words about a place in between. Electricity substations, long boarded-up sheds, lock-ups, someone else must have a key for that. Someone, somewhere must have a key for that. The miniature mysteries and everyday places you don't question.

When Darren got home he was so agitated he almost felt like running again, but he was still shivering from the cold sweat, and his muscles had stiffened, so he ran a hot bath. From the bath he called Helen.

'Listen, I've got a Latin question for you. Vade In Pacem. It means go in peace, right? But does it mean anything else? Any reference I should know about?'

'Vade in Pace, or Vade in Pacem?'

'Pacem, definitely.'

'Then it's not a peaceful saying. Rather than go in peace, it means go into peace. Go inside, into peace. It's a punishment. It was used in the sentences for nuns who had broken their vows. Well Darren, you have really creeped me out. Tell me this is about your paper on anchoresses, and not about the Wild

Woman case?'

'I'm in enough trouble with Colette already, I'd better not say anything. I'll let you know when I can. Thanks.'

That night Darren dreamt of the manhole cover, and felt dizzy in his dream. The manhole as the still point in the turning world, the anchor, the fulcrum. He dreamt of being trapped in there himself. Jumping to try and reach the ladder that was just out of reach. Clawing at the walls.

He felt no satisfaction; only a strange sense of having uncovered something that had been hidden for a long time, a strange sense that perhaps it should have remained hidden. Why did he feel like this?

A reality was beginning to construct itself around the narrative he had created. He imagined Diane running through the park in blind terror, hiding in bushes, snagging her dress on gorse, forcing her wasted muscles to hoist herself over the fence in a last superhuman effort.

Chapter Twenty-Six

Helen had been summoned to see the head of the Religious Studies department. This was a rare event, since outside of their monthly departmental meeting she was usually left to her own devices. She gave her own lecture series on Eschatologies, and taught the core first-year curriculum which hadn't changed in all the years she had worked there. So she wasn't entirely sure what this was about, but she had a suspicion it might be a promotion, and knocked on the door of Professor Henry Knowles, head of the Theology Department, with breezy confidence.

'Ah, Helen, come in.'

Professor Knowles was an old-fashioned academic who had never quite adapted to life outside the Oxford college from which he had been promoted to head of department in Liverpool. His teaching room may not have had the oak panels, the scent of pipe smoke and sherry, or the weight of centuries, but he had still managed to create for himself a little nest of scholarly chaos. While buses roared by outside and skyscrapers encroached on the view, inside, every surface, including most of the floor, was piled with books, manuscripts and papers. Helen had to pick her way to the chair waiting for her across from his desk, at which he was marooned, a sinking ship in an ocean of printed words.

He was kind and tolerant but chronically disorganised and Helen imagined he loathed his administrative and management duties, hence his normally laissez-faire attitude. As soon as she sat down, she realised this was not going to be a promotion. His face betrayed irritation and embarrassment, and he fumbled with a pen and shuffled papers absently, hiding his eyes behind thick glasses and bushy eyebrows.

'Well, this is awkward. You've been here, what? Eight years.'

'That's right. Nine actually.'

'Our novelty nun. Until last year when you suddenly became a…' He nodded at her appearance, struggling to find the words. When she had first stopped wearing her habit, she had dressed in the conservative floral dresses and shoes that she had kept from her teens. But gradually she had developed her own style; or rather, she had taken on Mikko's, and today she wore a Total Depravity t-shirt and a pair of his combat trousers which had various chains needlessly hanging from them. She felt this was as much a uniform as her habit and veil had been before.

'… a rocker, are you? A biker?'

'A lay person.'

'Quite. But really, we've not had a peep out of you. Until now.'

'Oh?'

'We've had a couple of complaints. Two in a week, in fact.'

Helen's face fell. Was this about Amber Rees? She had after all got into that lab under false pretences. Or was it about her relationship with Darren? Perhaps it had been noticed that they went for coffee together after every lecture. Maybe it wasn't appropriate to single out one student for friendship. Or perhaps it was about Mikko, who had been hanging around the university recently. There were plenty of her students who were deeply religious and would be offended by the slogans on his clothing and various body parts.

'A Father Angelo Zotti called me. Said you've been… harassing him.'

Ah, so that's what it was. She felt a sort of perverse thrill to be at war with this abbot, but at the same time, she wasn't used to being in trouble.

'Harassment is a dangerous word, Professor. I hardly think…'

'But you don't seem that surprised,' he said, looking at her over the rims of his glasses, his bushy eyebrows raised.

'I hardly think it constituted harassment. Let's say haranguing.' *Why did I say that?* she immediately thought.

'You can't invite someone as a guest speaker and then interrogate them, create a hostile atmosphere, follow them out of the building. It's bad for our reputation.'

She sighed. 'I'm sorry. I don't really know what got into me.'

'I imagine Father Zotti and everyone else knew what had got into you. You've clearly got unresolved issues related to your own time as an enclosed nun. But taking it out on a local monk in a public forum is not the answer. Go and see a therapist, or whatever you young people do nowadays.'

'I'll write to Father Zotti to apologise. You said there was another complaint?'

'Oh yes. You've been... going off script. You gave a first-year lecture yesterday on the apocrypha. And some very fastidious student came and complained to me. Now I'd be the first to admit that's all very interesting – the apocrypha is my specialist subject - but it's simply not on the curriculum, and it wasn't the scheduled lecture. So, I had a look through your recent publications.' He flicked through the pile of papers, which she realised was a collection of her works. Perhaps this was more serious than she thought.

'Your recent publications: 'The Quest for Gnosis in Slovenian Black Metal'; 'Druids, Death Metal and the Construction of Esotericism'; 'Liturgical Commentaries on Punk', 'Interpretations of the Apocalypse in Thrash Metal'; Occultism and Feminism in 1920s London.' That's all very well, and you're nothing if not prolific, but our students simply didn't sign up to study music or feminism.'

'But many people signed up to follow my Eschatology course. It's the personal touch.'

'Yes, but until a year ago your Eschatology course hadn't so much as mentioned rock music – now you've got a whole lecture on it.'

'Yes, it's very popular. "The sacred and the profane: Music as a Religious Experience."'

'That's fair enough, but attendees would be expecting Bach, not Black Sabbath. We appreciate how consistent you've always been on the publishing front, but recent papers have been esoteric to say the least. We're a liberal department here as you know, and we cover all religions, but you have been, let's say, stretching the boundaries of theology.'

'It's true that I have developed some new academic interests recently. But that could be a good thing, don't you think?'

'Oh, absolutely. But you appear to be following your own agenda, Helen. And what that agenda might be, I wonder if you even know yourself.'

'Can I ask you something? What do you know about the Liverpool Natural Philosophy Society?'

'Dear God, you're not planning to invite that James Absalom chap as a guest speaker, are you?'

She smiled as she shook her head. 'No, I just… one of my students expressed an interest in joining the society, and I was a little embarrassed that I didn't know anything about them. We don't have any links, do we?'

'Goodness me no. They make a big deal about how they have been here longer than us. But there's no academic rigour that I've seen. That Absalom chap - there's an anti-intellectualism about him – despite his verbal virtuosity. You know when people say something so convoluted that it's impossible to tell if it's nonsense or not? That's his modus operandi.'

Helen smiled. 'That happens in academia all the time.'

'I suppose it does indeed. Anyway, he invites any Tom, Dick or Harry who has an opinion to his events, and then pits them against each other, like bear-baiting. A former colleague of mine was on recently, and he was absolutely annihilated. The mistake he made was thinking he could rise above the format. But you can't rise above the format.'

'I suppose it's like those ageing celebrities who go on those reality shows, thinking it will revamp their career. It can only end in humiliation. Unless the programme-makers decide otherwise.'

'Well I wouldn't know about reality shows. But what people want to see is humiliation. A scapegoat for all the humiliations in their own life. If I was your student I would be careful about getting involved with that Society. There are good reasons why we keep them at arm's length. It's not intellectual snobbery, although of course, that is what we are accused of and we can't win.'

'Isn't it intellectual snobbery?'

'Well, if maintaining rigour and dignity is snobbery then yes, I suppose it is. Their mythical book collection – they guard it almost gleefully. I wonder if there is anything in there at all.'

'What do they say is there?'

'The private collection of William Merchant. He was one of the first great antiquarians. The earliest merchant ships going between Liverpool and the middle-east, with the first biblical treasure seekers on board. Merchant was probably barely literate, but this was all about status. There's no denying what he started - the beginning of the golden age of Liverpool. He wanted to prove he had arrived by becoming a cultural patron, and in that respect, he did a great service to the city, because others followed.'

'But if his collection is as special as the myth they have created about it, it should be in the hands of the British Library, or at least available – for their protection. Public Goods.'

'Indeed. But the collection is privately owned. And apparently members are remarkably loyal.'

'Do you think they really have anything?'

'Oh, it's very possible. In the early seventeenth century, the first wave of antique manuscripts coming in from the Middle East would have arrived at the port of Liverpool, and William Merchant would have been as likely as anyone to get his hands on them. At the same time, however, there were a lot of fakes being bandied about at the time. It was a very common Elizabethan joke to write fake prophecies and so-called found texts. People were mourning the loss of the magic of Catholicism, and were looking for answers. So, they were vulnerable to pranksters. And then of course the horror of the Civil War seemed to confirm the fire and brimstone prophecies being bandied about.'

'Even a fake would be fascinating, wouldn't it? What I wouldn't give to get into that library.'

'Well, please don't give your job – by getting yourself into trouble. Stick to the curriculum, if you would, Dr Hope. Very good.'

As Helen got up, she noticed a Guardians Of Truth leaflet on top of Professor Knowles' messy inbox.

'Do you know the Guardians Of Truth?'

'Know of them? Yes of course. They are the offspring of the Northern Methodist movement which has been around since the Reformation. But it's all rock concerts and mass baptisms and happy-clappy stuff nowadays. More your sort of thing than mine.'

'Not exactly. I thought of inviting their leader Jared Case to be a guest speaker.'

'Another terrible idea, Helen. They are evangelical and we don't want to be accused of trying to convert people to anything. You're as bad as James Absalom if you invite a creationist here. It's such a minefield out there.'

'Yes, it is. Life was certainly simpler in my convent.'

'Well stop trying to make my life more complicated by inviting inappropriate guest lecturers. Fix your own lectures first, alright? Off you go dear.'

Chapter Twenty-Seven

Easter Sunday came, and Darren was more aware than he had ever been of what it meant. He remembered very clearly the Easter celebrations with his parents at the Mainstreet Church. Although celebration was hardly the right word. As a young child he had been terrified and impossibly sad at the brutality of the crucifixion, found it unfathomable that no-one else seemed to have nightmares about it. And then as an adolescent he found it risible, absurd, that this gruesome murder story could possibly be the basis for a religion.

And then after he had left home, and throughout his adult life, Easter had meant nothing more than the shops being full of chocolate, and a long weekend of drunkards to be policed in the city centre.

Now the crucifixion was on his mind, the resurrection, the whole story. He still couldn't quite get his head around it, even after Helen's lecture of the subject.

Thomas had flown to Madrid – in secret – for talks with the new club. And Darren had not gone with him. Now back from his run and with the whole day stretched ahead of him alone, he flicked on the television, where the local channel was showing the Easter service at All Angels' Church. Darren smiled when he spotted the camera pan over Mikko amongst the congregation, his mouth moving to a hymn.

Helen had always loved Easter. Even the sound of the word, the 'Passion', had always filled her with excitement. She had loved the magic and horror of the story that brought the Bible to life for her. In position with her church choir at All Angel's, she looked at the stained glass that depicted the crucifixion, and stole a glance at the giant wooden cross behind her. Christ's expression of agony, his crumpled, broken body, the blood pouring from his wounds. She sang out loud with her choir, but her head was somewhere else, and she was unable to concentrate on the service today.

If Owen was the next anchor, then the day of the crucifixion would be his initiation. Monastic initiates were always confirmed at Easter, it was tradition. And then it might be too late. But she had nothing to go on other than her paranoia.

April – the season of new life coincided with the all-consuming memory of Christ's brutal death – one of Christianity's most harsh paradoxes. It had always somehow felt right to her, but now it felt wrong. Somehow nothing made sense anymore. She spotted Mikko at the end of a middle pew, sharing a hymn book with an old lady. His mouth was vaguely moving but he was looking around the church, like a child, in mild, absent wonder. How bored he must be. She felt embarrassed, but he had insisted on accompanying her.

They were about to go and perform at a festival which promoted creationism. Young, educated people, who genuinely seemed to believe, and promoted the notion, that the Earth was only four thousand years old. How could people live with that cognitive dissonance? How could they deny the facts? But then, perhaps it wasn't all that different from her faith. Perhaps her Christianity was cowardly, cherry-picking as she did the parts of the Bible she could live with. All of it was starting to feel more absurd and far away.

The choir sang 'Tell Out My Soul', the hymn of the Magnificat, which told of Mary's visitation to her cousin Elizabeth, using the words of the Gospel of St Luke. It wasn't strictly an Easter hymn, but since the television cameras were there she had decided to choose their best numbers. This had always been her favourite hymn anyway, and she liked to sing it at Easter because she imagined it would have been around this time of year that Mary discovered she was pregnant.

The choir soared through their melodies, harmonies and counterpoints. Helen always liked to imagine the scene; Mary congratulating her cousin on her pregnancy, putting her hand to Elizabeth's belly and feeling the baby, the future John the Baptist, move inside, knowing that she herself was pregnant with the Lord. Helen put her hands to her own belly. She often did this while singing, to regulate her breath. She realised that her period was late. Very late.

'Right lads, are you listening? Colette's got a probable ID on the 1990s skeleton.'

At Crosby police station, meeting room two was occupied by Operation Wild Woman, as Colette, Dave and Baz had called themselves. McGregor was becoming increasingly involved due to the media interest in the case, and he was over from Canning Place for the afternoon. He sat on the desk and watched Colette's presentation.

Darren had been right so far about the wild woman, so Colette had taken his advice on the search for the bones' identity. When she had looked for missing persons in Blundellsands, she came up with nothing. No-one ever disappeared from Blundellsands. They didn't leave. Who would leave, when it was all about arriving?

But Darren had suggested trying something else. To get the records of Keystone House, and look for anyone who was a resident there in the 1990s who went missing, after they left. And he suggested narrowing it down to the mid-90s, which made her search much easier. This latest skeleton was that of a woman in their mid-to-late thirties, with little sign of osteoporosis, meaning that if she had been imprisoned, it wasn't for a period of many years before Diane. Colette tried to ignore the fact that all this was based on a far-fetched theory about serial imprisonments lasting over centuries, and weird historical cults. Because otherwise it was like looking for the proverbial needle.

'Teena Rajpar,' said Colette, showing an image on the projector of a pretty young woman wearing a sari. 'I think this is her skeleton. Why? Because the timing fits. It sounds like this was a very sad case. Killed her own baby. It sounds like a case that would today would have been diagnosed as postnatal psychosis. But less was known about it back then, and she was charged with manslaughter on the grounds of diminished responsibility. Nowadays she would have received more care, psychiatric care, but in 1985 she was sent to Styal Prison. Released on probation in 1992, at the age of thirty-two, spent a year at Keystone House. Released back into her family's care in 1993, never heard from again. Registered as a missing person in 1994, for reasons I haven't discovered yet, but the case was dropped.'

'Can we find this family?'

'We need to find them, to identify the body.'

'They're not going to identify a skeleton, are they?'

'No, but it has a distinguishing feature. A leg broken in adulthood. Maybe they can confirm that.'

'It's a long time ago… I hope they are still around.'

'It looks as if her husband moved to Canada in 1987… but his brother still lives in Liverpool, near Rainford.'

'Alright, nice one,' said McGregor, 'we can drive over there now. What else have we got? What about this Tony Norris character?'

'Tony Norris has a sort of alibi. He was in Australia the whole of last year visiting family. While that doesn't rule him out of messing about with those skeletons or releasing Diane, there's no way he was around to be keeping her alive until then. And he didn't have a park key.'

'But if we can find a connection between Keystone House and the private park we might have something.'

'The monks - they've always visited Keystone House, always had a Hawthorne Park key.'

'Yep. That's all there is though – it's circumstantial. There're probably others who fit that profile. But we're definitely centring this on Keystone House now. Go through the records – board members of the foundation past and present, park key holders and foundation members, past and present. See what comes up.'

Chapter Twenty-Eight

At the Rajpar house in Rainford, they had interrupted a family party. Mr. Rajpar, the brother-in-law of Teena, only allowed them in after silent cajoling from his wife. Colette and McGregor sat in the pristine living room, an atmosphere of low-level hostility not just because Mr. and Mrs. Rajpar were anxious to return to their grandchildren who were running around in the garden, but also because this was a painful topic to which they did not want to return.

'We wanted nothing to do with her as a family,' dismissed Mr Rajpar. 'After what she did.'

'She disappeared without a trace,' nodded his wife, placing a comforting hand on his knee.

'She will have gone back to her family in India.'

'Mr Rajpar,' said Colette, 'we have reason to believe that one of the skeletons found in Crosby is that of Teena.'

'If you are implying it was her husband who did it, it's not possible. My brother moved to Canada before she got out of prison.'

'We're not implying anything of the sort. But if you believed she had gone back to India, why did you register her as a Missing Person?'

'I didn't. No way. I don't know anything about that,' he said. 'And I'd like to go back to my grandchildren now.'

Colette's notes said otherwise. Teena had undoubtedly been registered as a missing person in 1994. But she noticed the discomfort of Mrs. Rajpar, so she decided to move on. There was more to this.

'We'll see ourselves out,' she said, and she had a feeling that Mrs. Rajpar would follow.

'Detectives," she called after them, and stepped outside, closing over the front door furtively behind her. 'It was me who registered Teena as missing. He... does not know. He was in Canada at the time, visiting his brother.'

She spoke urgently, anxiously, in a hushed voice, looking over her shoulder frequently. Eventually she closed the front door behind her and walked out to the car with them.

'The rest of the family shunned Teena. I have a lot of sympathy with their position. She killed Ayaan's son. But she had severe postnatal psychosis. She loved that child more than life itself, but she wasn't herself. She was a twenty-year-old girl, thousands of miles from home, with a husband she had only just met. I knew what that felt like. So, I visited her in secret, in prison, and then at the half-way house. When she left, I also assumed she had gone back to India, but when I tried to contact her after a year, her family had had no word from her. So that was when I... but there was no interest in the case.'

'Mrs Rajpar, do you think Teena was murdered by a family member, as revenge for what she did?'

She looked horrified. 'No! My goodness, no,' she whispered, looking behind her anxiously. 'We are a loving, grieving family. Nothing like that. There just wasn't the same understanding of these issues back then.'

'So, what do you think happened?'

'What I wanted to tell you was this. When Teena was at that half-way centre, Keystone House, she changed. She became calm, accepting, she said they were helping her and she had found a place she could go. I didn't know what she meant, and then when I lost touch I just assumed...You know I had small children of my own at the time, I couldn't keep track. When did she die?'

'If it's her, 1995.'

'Then where was she, for two years?'

'Somewhere near here, it seems.'

Colette and McGregor got back into the car and drove off. McGregor tapped the steering wheel incessantly in frustration.

'Something happened at Keystone House. Something was going on that resulted in the violent death of Teena Rajpar, and the kidnapping and eventual suicide of Diane Goodwin.

Chapter Twenty-Nine

'Those crosses are the wrong way round.'

From their vantage point in the bus park on top of the hill, Total Depravity and Helen surveyed the festival that was laid out before them. Truth Fest had been lucky with the weather, and it was shaping up to be a fine, sunny day, unseasonably warm for May.

The Total Depravity tour bus was parked next to Sporn's two luxury coaches, with a series of lesser vans parked alongside. To their left was the campsite, and the festival itself was laid out on the slope, a food truck area to the left, a lesser stage to the right, and everything leading up to the main stage, where a rapper was performing. At each side of the stage was a giant cross, that flashed in different colours as the main part of the light show.

'This is actually my first ever music festival,' said Helen.

'The first of many,' Mikko said, putting his arm around her shoulders. 'Hopefully your next one will be Wacken, because this one kind of sucks. I mean look at that tagline. I can't believe we have to play underneath that.'

Above the main stage was a huge electric scrolling sign with the festival's slogan 'It's All Good' followed by a smiling 'halo' emoji.

'That is some real bullshit.'

'It is rather Panglossian isn't it,' she smiled.

'It's - what do you call it - a thought-terminating cliché. Because what can you say to that? It's unfalsifiable.'

'Yes, it is quite offensive. Well, it's too late to back out now.'

'It is what it is. There's another thought-terminating cliché for you.' He left her standing there and went to sit on the steps of the bus where he began rolling a cigarette on top of a crate.

Mikko was moody. Helen wondered if he was regretting this festival, their relationship, everything. She felt a disconnect between them, and she couldn't put her finger on it, nor did she know what to do with it. He was usually so easy-going, but the past few days he had been on edge, and now he had almost snapped at her.

Her phone buzzed in her pocket, and when she looked it was a text from Darren: *I've been accepted into the Natural Philosophy Society! Got my initiation tonight!*

Ok, if you're sure… she replied.

Knut appeared looking pleased with himself in a t-shirt that proclaimed 'Jesus Is My Brand'.

'That goes well with your tattoos man,' said Mikko, fist-bumping him.

Helen sighed, feeling complicit in something although she couldn't quite define its wrongness. And that indignance gave her confidence – they were in the wrong here, and if she professed her indignance she could tell herself she was less complicit.

'Don't you think you should wear a hat just for this weekend, Knut? It really couldn't be any more offensive.'

Knut just grinned. 'Oh, it can get much more offensive, you will see.'

Helen wondered if he was really going to spend the rest of his life with an inverted cross tattooed on his forehead. She dreaded what they were going to do on stage.

'Oh look, there's the guy.'

Mikko pointed with his cigarette, and they all turned around to look at the main stage. There was a roar of applause as Jared Cage appeared, and he bathed in the cheers for several prolonged moments, putting his hands to his heart in a gesture of humility.

Although the stage was several hundred metres away from their position, they could hear him clearly over the festival speakers. He was announcing a mass baptism that would be taking place the following morning at the lake. This spectacle was to be the culmination of the festival. The crowd raised their hands to the sky, and Helen noticed that the only difference between this and a heavy metal crowd was that their palms were open and didn't make the devil horns gesture.

'Well, I suppose I had better round up the girls and get ready. We're on soon.'

The All Angels Choir performed at midday on the breakout stage, the smaller stage that lay at right angles to the main stage. Even with her lack of festival experience, Helen knew this was a graveyard slot. They had only a sporadic crowd. Mikko and the rest of Total Depravity dutifully watched them, whooping and raising their hands in metal horns gestures. If she had been in a better mood, she would have smiled back at them, because she knew they were only trying to make her smile. But instead she felt a little humiliated, patronised.

Later on, Helen loitered around the bus park; for some reason she couldn't define, she wanted to stay away from the festival itself. She had been watching with interest the comings and goings from Sporn's tour bus. Unlike the powerful, charismatic on-stage persona she had watched on YouTube – the heavy metal evangelist who was said to have converted thousands to Christianity - in real life Rex Molina appeared to be a rather fragile figure. He had the slightly confused expression and mannerisms of someone on whom decades of drugs and alcohol had taken their toll. He wore a customised nylon shell-suit and was ushered here and there by his wife, who fussed and gave orders. It was clear simply from the body language over there who was in charge.

The woman had big blonde Eighties-style hair, and along with her stiletto boots she wore the timeless heavy metal fashion of leather trousers and denim waistcoat covered in vintage patches. Helen guessed that she must be around fifty years old, given the slight wrinkles and age-spots on her tanned, tattooed arms and neck, although both she and Rex had the slightly unnerving, surprised expressions that told of cosmetic work.

Helen realised that she had more than a passing interest in this woman. Was she herself the equivalent of Rex Molina's band wife? Would this be her future, if she stayed with Mikko, and was that a good thing or a bad thing?

The Sporn crew were keeping themselves to themselves, which was disappointing to Helen because she loved the Southern drawl of their accents. She supposed that they had done this festival thing thousands of times and had no need of or interest in making friends. But she got the impression that Rex had wanted to come over a few times, had looked sort of longingly in their direction, but had been prevented, protected from doing so. And so, Helen made it her mission to speak to him, or to this woman, and she found her opportunity that afternoon while Total Depravity were doing their sound check.

The afternoon had provided a rare sun trap and the woman was sitting on the steps of the Sporn bus, a notepad and stack of papers in front of her. She seemed to be editing something, and Helen noted with interest the stack of books next to her, one of which was a Bible. She chewed her pen and occasionally scribbled or underlined, occasionally raised her face to the sun and basked a little.

Helen wandered over. Surely this was the friendly thing to do, right? Since they were all in this together…

'Lucky with the weather, aren't we?' she said. The woman took off her sunglasses and blinked at Helen a few times before smiling. 'Hi', she said in an irresistible Deep South accent.

'I'm Helen, I just thought I'd come over and say hi. I'm…' *What am I?* she thought, and considered saying she was a performer, which she was of course. 'I'm with Total Depravity.'

'Aha. A fellow band wife. I'm Crystal.' She raised up her hand to shake hands. Helen shook it and then sat down awkwardly on an upturned beer crate, wondering if she should. But the woman seemed to accept.

'You know,' she said, wagging her pen at Helen's bus. 'Total Depravity was a strange choice by the festival for our support act. I gotta tell you, we started to have second thoughts.'

'Oh yes, I can totally understand. I'm not quite sure what we're doing here myself.'

'So, are you one of them Satanists then?' Crystal asked, continuing to scribble with her pen half-heartedly as if to dilute the intensity of the question.

'Oh, no! I'm actually a committed Christian.' Crystal just looked at her and blinked a few times, before saying 'You got a funny way of showing it,' and motioning to her Total Depravity t-shirt.

'It's hard to explain. It looks like you're busy here. Do you help Rex with his scripts and lyrics?'

'Help him, that's one way of putting it. I write the damn things. All of them.'

Crystal looked a little resentfully guilty, as if she probably shouldn't have made this confession, but was desperate to tell someone. 'I don't get no credit for it, but I write every single word he says.'

'Wow. Then you have a wonderful talent for explaining God's word. His performances are so inspiring.'

'Well, sometimes I guess it's easier to see these things from the outside. You can be more objective, I guess.'

This time it was Helen's turn to blink.

'Are you saying you're not religious?'

'Oh hell no. Pardon the language. I'm a bona fide atheist. I tried to believe, but I never could.'

'It's very convincing, then, what you do. No-one would ever guess.'

'I'm fully aware of the irony. Is it irony? I never really knew how to use that word properly. Rex is real dyslexic. Anyway, I write the words, and he interprets them. It's not like I ever finished high school neither, but I don't know, I just don't seem to find it hard to come up with this stuff. Between the Bible, and all the Oprah shows I been watching my whole life, you can come up with this Chicken-Soup-For-The-Soul type stuff that just speaks to people. It's not rocket science but, I don't know, I think I enjoy it. I was never much good at anything before. And Rex just *knows* how to say it so that it hits people in the right spot. We're a good team.'

'I couldn't help noticing the books you are using. I'm a theology lecturer.'

'Oh yeah, well we're coming up to our tenth year on the road, and people don't want to hear the same sermon every time. In fact, they wanna hear a different sermon every time – we make as much money from YouTube as from these gigs. So, I figure at some point I will have mined the Bible as far as it can go. I mean, it's a big book, but there's a lot of full-on bullshit in there, am I right? So, I started moving on to other scriptures. It gets real Da Vinci Code, I mean there's a lot of weird shit you can find.'

'I'm very interested in the apocrypha actually.'

'The apocrypha?'

'The other books… the ones that didn't make it into the Bible.'

'Right. Exactly. Apocrypha. That's a great word.'

'Try St. Augustine's Confessions. I recommend it. Oh, and the Book of Enoch. It's quite… metal, I suppose. Lots of fire and brimstone.'

Thanks, baby, I will. By the way, I hope you'll keep it on the down-low, about me writing the scripts. I can't believe I told you all that. And I don't even know you.'

Helen nodded and grimaced apologetically. 'I do seem to have that effect on people. They tell me things.'

'That's a pretty useful talent you got there.'

'I used to be a nun, so people feel strangely compelled to confess their secrets to me.'

'A nun. Jeez. Well, you got my confession, I guess. And it's a pretty expensive one, if any journalists find out.'

'Your secret's safe with me.'

'I believe it is.' Crystal looked at her for a long time, and Helen was hoping she would ask her if she had any secrets of her own. She was dying to talk to someone, especially another woman. But Crystal evidently had no time for making friends on the road. 'You have a good show out there with your devil-worshippers,' she said.

It was clear the conversation was over. And in any case, Helen wanted to go and ponder what she had just heard. What did it mean, if the world's most successful preacher was speaking the words of an atheist? Was her faith being exposed as a lie? Was it waning?

Chapter Thirty

'Right, where are we?'

Colette had had the flower pot swept for prints, but nothing came up. It had been touched by too many other people by the time it arrived in Diane Goodwin's hotel room. And the knife came up with nothing, other than Diane's own prints. The MyFlowers delivery had been ordered on April 7th by an independent florist in Bootle, called Bloomers. The florist had had no CCTV inside, only the owner's memory that a woman in a baseball cap had come in to make the order, and paid in cash. Before that, she had spent a long time lingering over the flower displays. That must have been when she hid the knife, and she had been very insistent about precisely which pot she wanted to be sent.

Dave had finally got hold of some CCTV from outside the shop two doors down, and located the moment when the woman entered the florist. The image was grainy and nothing came up when they ran it through the database. Only someone who knew this woman personally could possibly have recognised her.

At Crosby police station, their discussions kept circling back to the monks. 'There are so many coincidences, there has to be something there,' said Dave.

'I know, but there's nothing concrete,' said Colette. 'No prints, no sightings, we need more. Not enough to get a warrant yet. It's hardly a crime to have a Hawthorne Park key. Wheeler was a fastidious gatekeeper, and he seems clean. No connection to Keystone House either. We can't get anything on him. So that implies that whoever was keeping Diane had a park key.'

McGregor rubbed his mouth, deep in thought. 'Cross-check Hawthorne Park key holders with anyone connected to Keystone House – board members, staff – going back thirty, forty years.'

'I did,' said Colette. 'One name came up. Dr. Charles Merchant. But he died in 2010, ten years ago. And it says his key was passed on to his son.'

'Still. What's his connection?'

'He was a visiting psychiatrist at Keystone House. Other positions held – school psychologist, St Joseph's College. Until his death. He lived in Blundellsands, but the house was sold when he died. Here – there's a eulogy on the Institute of Psychiatrists' website.' She read out from her screen.

'*Dr. Charles Merchant was an eminent clinical psychiatrist who early in his career contributed significant research in the fields of operant conditioning and reinforcement schedules. A student of B.F. Skinner, the father of operant conditioning, Merchant published several papers on the use of operant conditioning chambers, or Skinner boxes. A Skinner box isolates a prisoner – a pigeon or rat – and exposes them to carefully controlled stimuli in order to predict and control their behaviour.*

'Keeping a prisoner in a box and manipulating them into accepting it through rewards and punishments– what does that sound like?'

They looked at each other. Colette carried on reading. '*Later in his career, Dr Merchant withdrew from academic life, publishing nothing after 1980, in order to focus on his patients. He served as in-house counsellor to Keystone House from 1980 until his death, helping hundreds of ex-prisoners to reintegrate into society. He was also the beloved school counsellor at St Joseph's school from 1982 until 2001.* Does that give enough for us to pay a visit to St Joseph's?'

'Definitely. Here's a thing about St Joseph's. My nephew goes there.'

'How posh are you?'

'Keep that on the downlow.'

'But the point is, I've been there for school concerts and whatnot. So, I know the headmaster, and he's been there forever. He's part of the furniture, they can't get rid of him. He must be well over retirement age now. He would remember Dr. Merchant.'

'Right, let's pay him a visit, shall we? You can wave to your posh nephew.'

Chapter Thirty-One

There was a general movement of bodies towards the lake; from Helen's position on the hill she could see them swarming in that direction. The Total Depravity tour bus was still empty since they hadn't returned from their sound check. Out of curiosity mixed with a strange unease, Helen followed the crowd.

Down at the lake, Jared Case was standing on a platform in the water. He was wearing a white long-length shirt, with white loose trousers underneath and sandals. He was beaming and held out his arms, palms open. Had she not felt so uneasy she would have found it comical, so cartoonishly Christ-like did he appear.

There was something odd about this place, about Jared Case, and the fact that Mikko had been so determined to come here. It wasn't because of Sporn... Mikko had played at hundreds of festivals, alongside the biggest rock bands in the world, and Sporn was just another. So, what was she missing? Mikko and Jared had been video-calling each other a lot, far more than it seemed would be necessary, she thought, to organise his performance at the festival. They had even met up in person, and bizarre as it was to her, Mikko seemed quite taken with him.

'I have no doubt he's in it to fuck as many women as possible,' he had said. 'I mean, unlike a guitarist, who's in it for the music but gets to fuck women as a bonus,' he teased her, 'I think that is Jared's main motivation. But at the same time – man, does he make you feel good about yourself. When he's talking to you, you feel like you're the smartest person in the world. The only person in the world.' Helen wished she could make Mikko feel like that.

Lamb of God

A team of young people stood in the water before Jared, all with the same smiles, all wearing the red t-shirts of the Guardians Of Truth. A small army, she thought fleetingly, a bit like the catchers at a metal concert, ready to guide crowd surfers safely over the barriers. And alongside each individual helper, holding their helper's hand, stood a candidate for baptism. All of them wearing white shirts and red necklaces. Jared began to speak into the microphone.

'Over one hundred people have said "I want to be baptised, I want to commit my life irrevocably to Jesus." We thank you for the gospel, for the life-changing message of Jesus Christ. We praise you, Lord, that your power is real, that you are the life-changer, the one who washes away our sin.' He paused to look out at his flock.

'These are my favourite ministry moments, because I can see that sin being washed away. What a joy it is today to come and worship you, Lord. We pledge to dedicate every moment of our lives to King Jesus. In Jesus' name, amen.'

There were 'Amens' from the crowd, all of whom were smiling, some with eyes closed and tears streaming down their faces. Some were swaying, many had their hands in the air.

'Water baptism is an amazing way to show the world that you have been changed by Jesus. Baptism is an outward expression of an inward decision. Now you will know what it means to die with Christ. This lake is a grave. Sit down in the water, stare into the water, and picture in your mind everything you did in your past, every sin, every lie the devil has told you, every fear, every anxiety, every sickness.' His voice had lost its kind tone now and became impassioned, inflamed. 'My helpers, who are Jesus' disciples, will put you down in that watery grave, and you will leave in that watery grave everything you have carried from your past, and when you rise… when you rise….' He paused to allow for the cheers. 'The Heaven will open above you, and you will hear the spirit of God whispering to you, in you: "I am well pleased."'

Helen was shoved from side to side as festival-goers pushed past her to reach the shore and see the spectacle. People were cheering, crying, hands raised to the sky. A couple of years earlier, Helen might have found aspects of this beautiful. Today she felt only a strange irritation at this full-immersion spectacle. When she had looked into this church, she had hoped to find something negative, even though she didn't know why she hoped, or why she felt irritated. There was nothing about the content of Jared's speech that she hadn't heard before. And he was right, baptism was a sort of death, and it was a public display of your decision to follow Christ. The old life going into the water symbolised Jesus' death, the new life raised out of the water symbolised Jesus' resurrection. Corinthians 2.17: *the old is gone, the new has come.*

And then she saw something that confirmed her agitation. Two of the candidates for baptism looked very familiar. Mikko and Knut were standing side by side, each holding hands with a disciple, joking with each other and fist-bumping. She watched open-mouthed, in disbelief, as they allowed themselves to be lowered backwards into the water, and then came up, gasping and wiping their faces. Knut roared 'Yeeaahhh' and made the devil-horns gesture, while Mikko just smiled and looked at the sky. He looked so convincing, so earnest, that at that moment she hated him. Mikko and Knut hugged their respective disciples, the gigantic Knut almost crushing the shocked teen in the red t-shirt, before wading to the shore. Helen pushed through the crowd, and blocked Mikko's path so that he could only stand there, dripping wet, the white shirt plastered against his ribs. He looked afraid of her, and the congratulatory crowds that buffeted them on all sides faded into the background.

Their eyes met and then she stormed away, pushing past the crowds, hoping he wouldn't follow her and hoping he would follow her.

'Helen, wait.'

She was crying and she felt the cold water as he caught up and took her arm, and she spun around angrily.

'You're making this very easy for me,' she said bitterly.

'Making what easy?' He looked confused, and she realised he had no idea of the turmoil she had been in about her future.

'How could you do that? Getting baptised as a joke – you've gone too far. You've gone beyond too far. Especially if that was some sort of publicity stunt. There's only so much I can tolerate.'

'I know. I was hoping you wouldn't see that.'

'So, you lied to me as well.'

'No. Yes. I was embarrassed. I didn't know how to explain. But I need you to hear me out. Please. Remember when we first met? You came to me with some crazy story that made no sense? And remember when I agreed to listen, and went along with it? And… saved your life?' He winked. 'You owe me.' He smiled, and she didn't smile but she did agree to listen.

Chapter Thirty-Two

'The last time I was here, I was in the sixth form netball team,' said Colette, as they pulled into the car park of St Joseph's College. 'I remember we used to make fun of the uniforms they had to wear here. Blazers and straw boater hats and everything. We used to chuck sweets at their heads from the back of the bus.'

'Proper yobbo, weren't you?'

'The uniform hasn't changed one bit, look.'

They walked through the front grounds of the private school, the most prestigious in the city, like an Oxbridge college incongruously transported there. A bell was ringing for change of lesson, and flocks of purple blazers wafted past them. They were shown through oak-panelled corridors to the office of elderly headmaster John Patterson.

'I'm ever so sorry, I wasn't aware that he had died.'

'But I thought he worked here until his death?' asked McGregor.

'No, no. The truth is, he left under something of a cloud. It was a real shame as a matter of fact.'

'What happened?'

'He had been the school psychologist for a long time, done some great work. Really pioneering; of course, now it's much more common to have school psychologists, but we took an interest in young people's mental health long before it became fashionable. Anyway, his son joined the school at age eleven. He was a problem, and eventually he was suspended. His father disagreed of course, but after what he did there was no way we could allow him to stay, there would have been uproar from the parents.'

'What did he do?'

'Plagiarism. There are internet tools to catch it nowadays, so it's not so common. But if I remember correctly, he cheated on all of his exams. Not an original idea in his head. He probably wouldn't have passed the entrance exam to get into this school, but of course the children of staff got a dispensation back then. If my memory serves me, he was a bit of a fantasist. James, his name was, that's right. I believe he went off to boarding school in the end, Westcastle is where we used to recommend in these situations. And Dr. Merchant said his position here was no longer tenable.'

Back at the station, Colette couldn't find any relevant James Merchant on the internet. She called Westcastle School, who directed her to Oxford Brookes University, where she discovered that a James Merchant dropped out of his degree in 2012. She found his photo in the student union records and headed straight to McGregor's desk. 'You'll never guess who he is. It's that guy. I've seen him on TV.'

Darren was on his way to Horrox House when he received a phone call from Colette:

'Listen, I'm going to send you a screenshot from the CCTV outside the flower shop. It's too grainy for the software, but just on the off-chance you recognise this woman, let me know.'

She pinged over the image. 'It's difficult to see, but you can make out her hair and features. Not well enough to do any database matching. You don't happen to recognise her, do you?'

Darren held his phone in front of him to squint at the image, then put it back to his ear.

'Do you know, I think I do. And it confirms what I thought. Listen – remember what I said about tonight, ok?'

'I really don't like the sound of this, Darren.'

'It's the only way. Trust me on this.'

Chapter Thirty-Three

Helen and Mikko sat on top of a picnic bench at the edge of the parking lot. It was late afternoon and a chill wind had begun to blow. Before them was the mess of festival debris as the weekend drew towards its close. Overflowing waste bins, litter blowing across the ground, grass worn down to soil, discarded tents, tired bodies, stallholders packing up. The stages were empty, and bodies ebbed and flowed and moved between stalls and tents. It was a limbo period before the evening finale, with only the four main acts to perform now, including Total Depravity, right before the headliner Sporn. Helen shivered a little, but Mikko knew instinctively not to try and move closer to her. She leaned forward with elbows on her knees, hands clasped to her chin, and she felt utterly desolate, because this was probably the end of things. And yet – she placed a hand to her belly surreptitiously. What a mess.

Mikko tried leaning back to relax the atmosphere, but when it didn't work he leaned forward and mimicked her pensive position.

'What does this remind you of?' he said.

Eighteen months ago, they had sat on top of a similar bench at the edge of the M6 motorway, with the same Total Depravity tour bus parked nearby, and Helen had had a feeling of desolation then, but for different reasons.

She smiled grimly. 'Yes, except that time I was the one who had some explaining to do. How could you do that?'

He turned to face her and tried to take her hand, and she felt it would be so petulant to refuse that she allowed him.

Lamb of God

'I know you think that Knut and I just got ourselves baptised as a piss-take. And Knut... kind of did. I mean, he did. But... I didn't.'

'What do you mean? I saw you. And you were smirking.'

'I did get baptised, yes. But I meant it. I... started to believe.'

Helen looked out towards the sky which was now a blaze of colour. The wind had broken the clouds into a million pieces and each one had a metallic sheen against a pink washed background. She began to piece together her own fragments of possibility – the Bible he had been reading, his pensiveness recently, his conversations with Jared Case, and that smirk - perhaps it had just been a smile.

'All of that stuff that happened last year,' he said, urgently picking threads from the holes in his jeans. 'I mean there are some things that only made sense if – if there's something else out there. And I couldn't stop thinking about that guy in Monaco, you know, that billionaire asshole...'

'Laurent Baptiste.'

'Right. Remember what he said to us? That it's safer to believe in God, to hedge your bets? Well, it kind of made sense. It resonated, on a selfish level, you know? It's Pascal's Wager.'

'Yes, I know Pascal's Wager.'

'So, I decided to try it out. It started out as an experiment, a sort of intellectual experiment. Maybe I even wanted to get closer to you, I don't know. So, I tried doing it, doing religion. Just performing it, like a ritual. Reading the books, singing the hymns. And then, there comes a point when there's little difference between doing it and believing it. There was no sudden moment of revelation, no thunderbolt or anything... I just realised that I wasn't performing any more. It was doing something for me. I realised that it's ok to believe without proof. A leap of faith, right?'

'Why didn't you talk to me about it?'

'I don't know. I guess I was embarrassed. I mean, my brand is kind of the opposite of Jesus. I just needed to figure it out for myself. And then, I didn't really know how to tell you. So, I took the cowardly route of… I don't know… letting you see that instead. You know how we were talking about post-irony? The thing about post-irony is that you don't know if it's sincere or not. It can tip into sincerity. And that's how I got away with coming here.'

'You came here under false pretences.'

'Well, kind of. It depends on your perspective. I guess I was pretending to pretend.'

'So, you and Knut…'

'No – not Knut. He's taking the piss, and he plans to burn in Hell one way or the other. I haven't told him what I've been feeling. But I… I…' he took a deep breath and looked down. 'I was being sincere. Obviously, this place, this Guardians of Truth thing, it's not my church of choice… it's ridiculous. I'd probably get more of a kick out of your Deaconess Margaret. But I wanted to know what it felt like. To be baptised. And the opportunity presented itself.'

'It feels strange to me that you talked to Jared Case instead of me.'

'It was somehow easier to talk to a stranger. You know? And there is something cool about how nice and accepting these people are. They didn't even mind my tattoos, I mean look at this stuff, these symbols should be so offensive to them. Maybe it's good to just go with it sometimes. It's kind of ironic that you're mad at me for becoming a Christian.'

'Irony. I thought it was post-irony that you were doing these days.'

'Post-irony is the new sincerity. And here's some sincerity for you – I love you.'

'I… love you too.'

'You said it! So now I might be a Christian, now you love me,' he teased.

'No, it's not that. It's just… I think we're going to be ok, that's all.'

Chapter Thirty-Four

Darren felt more alive than he ever had before; more than when he had come out, more than when he had met Matt. He felt on the brink of some revelation, something that would make everything alright. When he had arrived at Horrox House he had expected an event of some sort. He had no idea how many there would be at his initiation; he could only picture faceless, solemn individuals. Absurd and frightening at the same time. But the place was quiet; the lights off downstairs. There was only James, who answered the door himself.

'Did I get the wrong time? I thought there'd be loads of people here.'

'All in good time,' James smiled, welcoming him in.

He decided to go with it. James led him up the grand staircase, into the empty bar area, and then ducked under the bar to serve them.

'I rarely drink, but tonight calls for whisky, don't you think? Here.' He handed him a whisky. Come, let's go into the office. Now the thing is, before you meet everyone, there are some things you need to know. Membership requires acceptance of certain truths, and I think you are ready to know them. I think you are ready to know the truth. Things hidden since the foundation of the world,' he said, grandly.

They sat down in the window seating area with the burgundy leather armchairs. On the low table between them was an old wooden box, and James opened it theatrically. Inside was a crucifix, in coloured wood depicting the Christ figure on the cross, and next to it a red necklace.

'The crucifixion. A fundamental turning point in human history; certainly, in the history of morality. And mankind relies upon a fundamental misunderstanding of what it means. The Passion – the violent death of a son at the hands of his father – was supposed to free humanity from their sin. It was supposed to be the ultimate sacrifice, the sacrifice to end all sacrifice. It's a lie. The lie on which humanity must base its morality. And the truth is… what do you think the truth is, Darren?'

'That God… doesn't require sacrifice. It's people that require sacrifice. To contain their violence.'

Absalom looked both stunned and amused. So much that he stood up, flinging his arms wide so that the whisky sloshed to the edge of his glass.

'You're completely wrong. It's the opposite. God requires continual sacrifice. It's in the book of... well, you'll see. The book that is missing from the Bible. For two thousand years we've been trying to explain away a snowflake nonsense. You can't make a God of jealousy and vengeance into a God of meek forgiveness. Think about it. What kind of a God would kill his own son? And in such a horrific way?'

'You're saying it didn't happen. It was humans that needed the sacrifice.'

'No, it did happen. Well, who knows? But what if it did happen? The clues were there… look at what God did to Abraham, to Job…'

Darren was feeling confused, but very very relaxed, and yet at the same time, on the brink of some revelation. Some warm revelation that would explain everything. He had the vague notion that there must be something in his drink, something was making him feel like this, but it didn't matter, didn't matter. Nothing mattered anymore but this.

'Come. It's time for you to see the library. I mean, the private library. It will explain more.' He continued to talk as he walked, turning around, animated. Darren felt inexplicably tired all of a sudden. They had only just sat down, hadn't they? Why did he have to get up again? But he felt he would do whatever James said.

'By making God good, the Gospels deprive God of his essential role in primitive religions – of being responsible for good AND evil. This is the lie – or the spin – of Bible hermeneutics. The clues are all there. What sort of a God would murder his own son? God is a vengeful God. The Old Testament God, full of wrath and cruel tests and vindictiveness, that is the true God. The New Testament is a cover up. The greatest conspiracy theory in history. In the gospels, violence is always laid at the door of humans. We stopped blaming God. But man was made in God's image, so why would God not be violent too?'

James continued to talk, but the words were washing over and around Darren. He felt he was floating in a thick, soupy ocean of words and concepts. James unlocked the plexiglass door into the main library, and then another door into the private area. There was an instant chill on Darren's face as the temperature dropped, rousing him slightly from his stupor.

Displayed on the dais, under another plexiglass box, was a frail, stained manuscript. There was an underlying humming in the room, which came from a dehumidifier and temperature controller. Was it that which was making his head spin?

'It's just fragments,' explained James, as they looked at the manuscript together. 'But they are fragments of a codex. You can tell by this edge here – this was a page stitched to a spine. A codex was the earliest type of book, which replaced rolls of papyrus or wax tablets. And this one is in fact older than the

Codex Sinaiticus – it's from the third century, which makes it the oldest book in the world. You see I wasn't lying when I said the British Library would kill to get their hands on this.'

Darren peered at it, holding the dais to keep himself steady, because that whisky was really kicking in. The writing was spindly, with leaned-back lettering in an alphabet that he didn't recognise.

'Is that Hebrew?'

'Aramaic. But it would be hard to decipher even if you could read Aramaic. There has been some acidic degradation, but the main issue is that it's a palimpsest.'

'Palimpsest?'

'It's been written on top of something else. It was a way of reusing parchment – very hard to come by in its time. Very expensive, so it was recycled. And that means that the original Codex was even older.'

'What's it about?'

'It's the Book of Barabbas.'

'Barabbas – the prisoner who was released instead of Jesus?'

'Indeed. The ultimate 'Where Are They Now?' figure from the bible. Those scriptwriters just wrote his character out. Or did they?'

'Sorry, you're losing me.'

'Like I said, it's the conspiracy to end all conspiracy theories. The parts that were left out of the Bible. You see, the idea of God requiring a victim, even his own son, is intolerable to the human mind. But what if it is true? Only some of us can handle this information. The Church Fathers decided upon the myth of a benevolent God, so they covered up anything to the contrary, and the Book of Barabbas was suppressed. Amongst many other books, no doubt. The Church Fathers decided to conjure up this new happy-clappy Christianity, where it's all love and forgiveness, and we're still peddling the myth today. Protecting people from the truth.'

Darren squinted at the text. 'What does it say?'

'You'll get the translation.'

James was still as animated as ever, but more reverent now. 'This was the book that William Merchant obtained in 1639. The book that blows the New Testament out of the water. And it is the foundation of the Natural Philosophy Society. We are the guardians of its truth. And this is the unmasking of all masks. Basically, Barabbas bottled it. What do you know about Barabbas, Darren?'

Darren knew who Barabbas was; the other prisoner at Golgotha, a criminal condemned to be executed alongside Jesus. But Darren didn't want to speak; he was too tired, and he was slurring his words. 'Pontius Pilate allowed the crowd to choose one prisoner to be released, and the crowd chose Barabbas over Jesus.'

'Exactly,' nodded James. 'But why? Why were the crowd allowed to choose one prisoner?'

'It was... like a pardon... a customary thing...'

'Indeed, but which custom? If we go back to the Old Testament, to Leviticus, it tells us that God has always required two sacrificial goats at Passover. One for the Lord, to be a blood sacrifice, and the other for Azazel, to be cast out into the wilderness, taking away sin. It had been done for thousands of years, and that didn't change with Jesus. Jesus and Barabbas were the two goats. Don't you see?

'Jesus was the blood sacrifice, and Barabbas was supposed to be cast out into the wilderness, to take away the sins of the world forever. But he bottled it. This book tells us that he sloped home with his tail between his legs, and lapsed back into society. And so, like Eve when she took a bite of the apple, he condemned humanity. Jesus fulfilled his role, so the first goat was done, and no more blood sacrifice was needed. But Barabbas broke his covenant, his contract with God, and God went ballistic, basically. He condemned Barabbas to return to the wilderness, and to find a successor to continue his line forever. The second goat sacrifice must persist until the Second Coming.

Lamb of God

'Do you get it now? The New Testament is a Biblical appropriation of history. John 11:50 said "*sacrifice one single victim in order that the whole nation should not perish.*" Well, that's bullshit. Because there were two victims. Jesus was the first goat, and Barabbas the second. There had always been two goats, one for the Lord, and one for Azazel. It's the scapegoat mechanism, and it's the foundation of human society.

'Let's think rationally about this. The Bible texts are only a fraction, and they were arbitrarily chosen. The First Council of Nicaea - the guys who put it together in AD325 – well, they picked and chose. The books in the Bible are only a few among many that could have gone in. And it wasn't down to the vagaries of chance – it was a cover-up job, the council that made the definitive Bible.'

Darren was feeling very unsteady and nausea was building. He hadn't been drinking whisky recently, but still, he should have had more tolerance than this. James was continuing to rant, and he tried to concentrate.

'Everyone knows this – everyone knows the Bible is an arbitrary and tiny fraction of a whole, so why do we cling to the lie? Because the truth is far worse.'

'Why does it have to be a secret?' asked Darren.

'Because humanity can't accept the truth. Humans are a bunch of absolute pussies. They don't want to know that their God is a God of violence and terror, a God who killed his own son. And it's such arrogance, to think that we are more sophisticated than our ancestors who did accept this. The sly hypocrisy and, and, and, and... dreadful condescension which so many people show when they dress up the Christian text to make it sweeter and more palatable to our period.' James paused, and his eyes flashed, as if a thought had just come to him. He tapped on the plexiglass cover. 'When you read it, Darren, you'll see why I'm so interested in Andrew Shepherd. Every generation has its own monopoly on a... a... a sort of cartoon apocalypse. But the real

212

apocalypse will be far more insidious. Like a thief in the night. And according to this book, it may be already here. The beautiful thing is that it may be science that has discovered the Second Coming. And what could be a more perfect expression of the values of our society?'

The image of baby Elizabeth flashed into Darren's mind, but it was vague; he was grasping at something he couldn't understand, not while he was weighed down underwater like this. So many of Absalom's turns of phrase, Darren was sure, he had also used in his television shows. Hiding in plain sight. The clues had been there all along. In a strange way Darren had never felt so lucid, yet he was absolutely helpless, physically and mentally.

James was holding him by the shoulder now. 'I think you can understand, Darren. I think you share our vision.'

And he did, he was powerless to resist.

'Here.' From a shelf James handed him a book, little more than a folder, on printed A4 paper with cardboard on the outside. 'This is your copy. There will be plenty of time for you to study it. But, essentially, it explains the process. How are you feeling about all this so far?'

'Confused. I... I thought you were an atheist.'

'Oh no. Atheists are even more determined to maintain the sacrificial interpretation of Jesus. What is really frightening today is not the challenge of this new meaning, but the Kafkaesque rejection of all meaning that is atheism. A panic-stricken refusal to glance, even furtively, in the only direction where meaning could still be found dominates our intellectual life. All the voices of our culture conspire to reassure us by discrediting the Christian text, and by avoiding it. And such hypocrisy, when we have placed on other myths! Oedipus! Our whole culture is based on that! And then we go searching for life on planets that we know to have been dead for billions of years.'

Darren had no idea how long James had been talking. Had it been minutes, or hours, or longer? He had lost his sense of time, and was completely disoriented. Was it dark outside?

'And without further ado, I think it's time for you to meet the rest of the Society, don't you?'

Chapter Thirty-Five

Helen watched from the wings as Total Depravity performed, and she noticed that her face was beaming automatically. She was smiling from ear to ear, and it was involuntary. He was magnificent on stage and she loved him, and how was this impossible situation going to end? At that moment she felt that she might do just about anything; do what Darren couldn't do and make a leap of faith. She was just as unsure as she had been when she took her vows, but somehow it was ok.

Mikko was probably doing more to convert people than anyone else at this festival, by the sheer power of his music, which had nothing to do with religion, and yet everything to do with religion. She watched the intensity of his expression as he rasped and growled into the microphone, his fingers moving like lightning across the guitar.

She had wondered what the crowd's response would be, to a band which had built its brand on hating religion. After an argument with Knut on the bus that had almost become heated, Helen had persuaded them to cut some of their more offensive songs from the set list, so they were left with the more palatable ones that were based on literature rather than blasphemy. But if there had been any doubts or hostilities, Mikko quelled them. In a far more honest echo of the *'who wonders about this Jesus thing'* line she had heard several performers toss out that weekend, he spoke into the microphone after their first two songs: 'We're here because we wondered about this stuff too. True belief isn't blind faith, it's about asking questions, thinking for yourself and drawing your own conclusions. And none of us have the answers.'

Later, she and Mikko watched Sporn together from the wings, enjoying the theatricality of Rex Molina.

He would pause for effect, one foot on a monitor at the front of the stage, nodding knowingly as he took in every face in the crowd, every plastic cup of beer held aloft, every hand raised in incongruent devil horns. He marched across the stage, as if he knew exactly where he was going. He would raise his hand as if clutching an orb, gazing at his stiff gnarled fingers in reverence. Jaw locked in a grimace, he looked out at the crowd, wrinkled eyes manic, hair and beard shaking. Then the eyes would narrow with knowledge, foreknowledge of a fundamental truth, he would nod slowly, and then speak. Voice rising and falling, sometimes a gentle cadence, here and there a sudden roar or a dash across the stage to point at some unsuspecting individual. And then with a spectacular pace change he would suddenly march to the other side of the stage, taking a Bible out of his back pocket and shaking it in the air before furiously flipping the pages. 'Let's go to Corinthians, verse five chapter ten: 'For we must all appear before the judgement seat of Christ, that each one may receive the things done in the body, according to what he has done, whether good or bad.'

And then he was in the zone, Bible back in his pocket, microphone back on the stand so that he can raise both arms to clutch furiously at invisible oranges in the air.

'Maybe you don't believe. But what if it was true? Hedge your bets, just for a moment, humour me. Jesus said "I am the light of the world. Whoever follows me will not walk in darkness, but will have the light of life." You gotta maximize your chances, brothers and sisters. This is not a drill. What if everything you do is being recorded, as it says in the Revelation about the Book of Life? Each of us writes this book of our own life. And we have the opportunity to repent, and receive forgiveness, and wipe those bad pages away. So that in the end, we will only have to account for our good works.'

And then he got everyone chanting. 'God is… great! God is… great! God is… great!' People started crowd-surfing up to the stage to receive Christ. It was almost out of control; the band played thrash metal while Rex blessed one flying festival-goer after another. There seemed to be more people in the air than standing in the crowd. Helen remembered what Crystal Molina had said to her back at the tour bus. 'I know what people say about us. It's a sideshow, a freakshow, whatever. But Rex has this unshakeable belief, no fear whatsoever. He always says, if just one person is inspired to look to Jesus, then it's all worthwhile. I don't care about Jesus, but I care about inspiring people.'

Helen had never been more confused about what she believed, but somehow, she had never felt more content.

After a couple of songs from Sporn's back catalogue, and a couple of Christian-themed new ones, Rex led the crowd in a mass rendition of the Lord's Prayer. The collective worship wasn't all that different from any other heavy metal concert she had seen. She found herself instinctively mouthing the words she had said so many thousands of times in her life, every day of her life. The Lord's Prayer was the prayer that Jesus taught his disciples, when they asked him how they should pray.

Our Father, who art in Heaven,
hallowed be thy name;
thy kingdom come;
thy will be done;
on earth as it is in Heaven.
Give us this day our daily bread.
And forgive us our trespasses,
as we forgive those who trespass against us.
And lead us not into temptation;
but deliver us from evil.

Lamb of God

For thine is the kingdom,
the power and the glory,
for ever and ever.
Amen.

Thy will be done. Thy will be done. Why did she keep thinking about that line? Thy will. Not my will. Of course. Because Jesus didn't want to die. The victim didn't have to be willing. Jesus begged his father, 'Please take this cup of suffering away from me...'

'Mikko,' she shook him. 'Thy will be done. All this time we've been looking for volunteers...'

'What? I can't hear you...'

'Oh my god. I have to call Darren... '

She ran from the stage wings, aiming for the back where she could just about hear herself. Darren wasn't answering his phone, so she called Colette.

'Colette, I think something very bad is about to happen to Darren. His phone seems to be off. But I think he's on Duke Street. Can you get there?'

'What... he told me not to worry. I am on Duke Street, I'm probably not twenty metres from him. But he told me he knows what he's doing...'

'What is he doing?'

'I don't know. But it doesn't feel right.'

Chapter Thirty-Six

'Here, let me top up your whisky before we go.'

James had taken Darren back to the foyer, they went behind the bar and James opened a door in the back wall. Darren found himself in the small hallway of an apartment decorated similarly to James' office. He imagined this must be the back half of the building, but he was feeling increasingly disoriented. The façade on Duke Street gave no indication as to how big this property was inside, and this was the edge of an area of industrial dereliction where one warehouse blended into another, some in use, some abandoned decades ago. There was no telling how far back it might stretch. In addition, he was feeling overly warm and his head was spinning. Yet he felt strangely relaxed.

They were in an apartment now, a stuffy, Edwardian apartment left over from when the frontispiece on Duke Street had been a real townhouse. They moved into a bedroom which was dimly lit, the windows covered by thick burgundy velvet curtains.

The room was spacious and grand enough for a four-poster bed, but instead there was a single hospital grade bed, empty, and next to the bed sat a very frail old man in a wheelchair. For a moment Darren thought it was Gerald Gardner himself, because he had the same shock of white hair and wizened, sinister, slightly crazed expression. But Gerald Gardner had died in 1964, and this man was supposed to have died in 2010. He wore the dandyish clothes that James had described his predecessor as wearing – a cream-coloured silk shirt with a ruffled neck, an embroidered frock coat and breeches. His clothes were in keeping with the room décor, but incongruous with the hospital bed, and the drip and monitoring machine to which he was hooked up. His mouth was slightly turned down, as if he had had a stroke. His hand quivered slightly.

Behind the man's wheelchair stood a young woman. Darren recognised her as the secretary, Nicole, who he had assumed was James' wife. He also recognised her as the woman with the blurred face from the florist's CCTV. By then, he hadn't been surprised. He had already made the connection.

'Darren,' said James, his hand on Darren's shoulder, 'this is my father, the eminent psychiatrist Dr. Charles Merchant. And my sister Nicole, who you've already met.'

'I thought you were dead.' Darren noticed that his own voice sounded faraway, as if he were underwater.

'I am dead, officially,' the old man croaked, speaking very slowly, every word an effort to pronounce. 'You can do a lot of interesting things when you're dead.'

Darren wasn't sure whether to move further into the room. He couldn't quite hear him. But as he moved forward he recoiled at the smell. The disinfectant had masked the stench of urine and must, and it smelled as if the man was rotting alive. When he stepped closer he could see the stains on the cream shirt.

'A living dead person. Did I want to experience it myself? Hold the anchor until Diane was replaced? Or am I a prisoner?' He motioned gruffly to his children. 'Am I a prisoner, or are they my prisoners? That is the question.' He began to laugh, but it degenerated into splutters and wheezes. Nicole fiddled with his oxygen and he settled.

'So, this is the one you've chosen, is it?' He pointed at Darren with a quivering, gnarled finger.

'Actually, Darren chose us,' James patted Darren on the back, and Darren looked at him questioningly. 'You came to us, remember? You asked to join. And you were the right age, filled with guilt - I had a good feeling from the start.'

'I didn't know what I was getting into.'
'No-one ever knows what they are getting into.'

Nicole looked blank. Vacant, but in a different way from the way Justine had looked vacant. Justine's eyes had had a sinister lack of empathy, that betrayed a knowledge of evil. Nicole looked drugged, as if she had numbed herself to her situation. Standing behind her father's wheelchair, the two of them motionless in the dim light were like one of the paintings, the staged portraits that lined the walls of the society's staircase.

Darren had a vague sense somewhere in his head that this was a bad situation, but he didn't feel worried at all - it must be ok because he had good instincts, didn't he? Did he have good instincts? He couldn't remember exactly why he was here, and felt very tired. He would have liked to sit down, very much, and wondered why they were still standing there. He was about to ask, but his jaw felt locked, as if speech would be a battle, like for James' father. He did remember that there was a reason he must stay awake.

'You're a damn fool James,' spat Charles. 'Four hundred years of work, about to come crashing down. And you've been keeping me alive to see it.'
'No, it won't, Dad.' James began to protest, gesticulating, in a petulant voice Darren had never heard, but then stopped himself, exasperated, then turned to Darren in his usual voice.
'I've always fundamentally disagreed with my father on this point. I think people need to know. It's a question of hermeneutics. We need this reminder of death. We need to know who is shouldering the burden.'
'He was a fool to let her go. You did it on purpose, boy, and you'll burn in Hell for it.'
'I did not let her go. I let my guard down, and she was up those

steps like there was no tomorrow. Well, strictly speaking there was no tomorrow for her, so what did she have to lose? I chased after her into the park but I suppose her night vision was better than mine. And then I thought, well, perhaps this is all part of the story.'

'The problem with this one is that he can't live in the shadows like the rest of us. Craves recognition. Validation. Product of his social media generation.' Charles spat those words out in disgust, staring at his son. 'Have you ever done anything without telling the whole world about it? What we do is the opposite.'

'Dad. We need to move with the times. This can be something else now.'

'Why don't you show him your new-fangled space then,' Charles muttered. James raised his eyebrows with elaborate pride, as if he was about to show him his new loft conversion or outdoor patio. But Darren felt he was approaching an answer. A danger, and an answer.

'Come on, Darren.' As they left the room, Darren noticed the bank of screens set up on the wall behind him, positioned so they could be watched from the hospital bed. He could vaguely see, in black and white, a series of images of a large empty space, shown from different angles, like security cameras. But there was no time to study it. He found himself being led down a corridor that ended with a door. And behind the door was a sealed circular metal vault, like the entrance to a giant bank safe. James continued to talk, turning back to him, sometimes pulling him up as he stumbled against the walls.

'Diane's release was a gift. Now we can take this to a whole other level, we can watch what happens. It really is ridiculous that we didn't do it before.'

James yanked a lever that opened the circular door.

'After you.'

Darren stepped through and then suddenly grabbed onto a wall with each hand, holding himself back. He was on a ledge around ten feet in the air. *It looks like an empty swimming pool,* he thought.

'It is,' said James, and Darren realised that he had said it out loud. 'It's much deeper than your average swimming pool though. I told the builders I was a diver.' And Darren retrospectively heard his own voice and it was slurred and strange. Suddenly he felt like laughing hysterically at the idea of drowning in an empty swimming pool. And he was laughing, and he hated the stupid sound of his voice, which made him laugh even more, and then suddenly he felt James come closer. For a moment he thought they were going to embrace, and then James whispered in his ear 'You're probably going to break something now. Sorry about that, but it's the best way,' and then he was shoved over the edge. He felt the crack in his leg, and just afterwards the clang of the security door slamming behind him. Then the agony brought him round somewhat from his stupor, and gave him a bit of clarity for a moment.

He was in a large cuboid room. There were no windows. The walls were bare concrete interspersed with mirrors, mirrors placed in order to reflect each other so that Darren could see infinite copies of himself. The overhead lights were like bright sunlight. There was a spartan mattress, a Bible, and an empty desk.

'So, what do you think?'

He heard James' voice and squinted up, to where James had appeared on a viewing platform that ran the length of the room, around twenty feet above Darren's head. Darren felt that he was laughing hysterically, but wasn't sure if it was only in his imagination. He had no idea whether his mouth was forming words and sounds or not. James shouted down and his words echoed throughout the space.

'I wanted a sense of absolute space – much more suitable for a wilderness than those holes in the ground. It's like a hall of mirrors. Stare into the abyss and the abyss stares back at you. With all the cameras and the viewing platform, I was inspired by the concept of the Panopticon. Designed by Jeremy Bentham.

The prisoner knows he or she is potentially being watched at all times. And of course, I was informed by my father's work on operant conditioning. You'll earn your rewards. It's completely soundproof, so don't waste your energy screaming.'

'Why... why are you doing this?'

'Despite what you might think, this is far more humane than anything that came before. Ever since the first time my father took me down that ridiculous oubliette in Hawthorne Park where Diane lived, filled with skeletons - absolute nightmare. I was determined to build something better. Despite what my father said, I don't crave recognition. Or perhaps I do. But I do fantasize about making this public one day. I even had the idea of writing it as a screenplay. Can you imagine the glorious irony of it? You know, I was going to move Diane here. I thought she would follow. That was my mistake, which I won't make again.'

'So, Diane Goodwin was the second goat?'

'Diane, and Teena before her, and the others before her. You will learn their stories, and you will write your own. Your visions will teach us much.'

Darren felt temporary bouts of lucidity, as his leg burned with pain, as if the pain was buoying him back up the surface now and again.

'Skeletons... why did you dump them?'

'I couldn't take them back here, there's CCTV everywhere, traffic cams, security cameras, I didn't want to risk it. And in any case, I'm planning this to be a more humane set-up. No more rotting corpses in the room, no contemplation of death all day, no open grave.'

'The whole place is a grave.'

'It depends on how you look at it.'

'I don't believe you. You could easily have got those skeletons here, or driven them somewhere far away, split them up. I think there's a part of you that wanted to be found.' Darren felt a little delirious. They were talking about this in such light terms. 'Was the line ever broken?'

'Oh, it hasn't been perfect. Keeping it within the family has had its challenges. But it was the only way. Do you know that the likelihood of a conspiracy being discovered is exponentially proportional to the number of people involved? And so, what a beautiful achievement, through the centuries. How arrogant of people to think we are more morally sophisticated than humans of the past? Does technological development equate with moral development? I think you knew, Darren. It wasn't coincidence that you found me. It wasn't coincidence you worked on the Shepherd case. It was serendipity, synchronicity, all that. It all fits.'

'So, do you work with those monks then, the Desert Fathers?'

'Ha, no. Very convenient though. The mystery behind the mystery, we are. Although they probably wouldn't be completely averse to our ways. What do you think the earliest desert fathers were doing, out in the wilderness? They knew. They knew the truth, they were just prevented from speaking it.'

James paused and smiled.

'You won't ever leave, Darren. You're mine now. And I think you wanted to be. No-one will look for you, because to them you have slipped off to be with Thomas. You have always burned bridges, and that's what we look for.'

Darren was slipping deeper and deeper. And as he faded, he relaxed into the knowledge that he had been right.

Chapter Thirty-Seven

In the dark van on the corner of Duke Street, Colette's fidgeting was uncontrollable. She was in the front seat with McGregor, while Dave and Baz were behind.

'He told us if we didn't hear from him by midnight, to go in.'

'It's 12.01. Are you sure about this?'

'I trust Darren.'

McGregor sighed. 'So do I. Bloody hell. Talk about ending my career in disgrace. Come on then.'

All his senses were blurred, and he had a vague sense of pain in his leg, but Darren became aware of a certain panic happening on the ledge above him. Nicole and Charles had appeared on the balcony too.

'What do you mean, the police?'

'I'm telling you, James, there are police cars outside. They won't stop ringing the doorbell. What shall I do?'

'Close off this area then let them in. This will be our first test. It's totally soundproof.'

'And your last test, James,' Darren found himself saying.

'What?' James laughed sneeringly, half-turning back to Darren on his way out, and then fully turning. 'What do you mean?'

'The police know I'm here.'

James had only a momentary panic. His face went through a series of expressions, which resolved into his go-to superiority.

'You asked me a while back, Darren, if there were other chapters of our society. Now you'll never know.'

He took a knife out of his pocket. Raised it above his chest with both hands. Closed his eyes in a brief prayer, and then did not plunge.

'I knew you wouldn't do it,' said his father.

At Canning Place, James Absalom sat in interview room one, Nicole Merchant in interview room two. The sister looked terrified, the brother looked… amused. Colette and McGregor were able to watch them both at the same time through the one-way glass.

'Well everything is fucking weird around here,' said McGregor, eating the sausage roll he'd been looking forward to since the early hours when they arrested the Merchants. 'It's like Darren Swift never left.'

Colette was quiet, and pursed her lips. It wasn't the time to tell McGregor that Darren had been advising her all along. At that moment Darren limped out of interview room three, the accompanying officer holding the door open for his crutches.

'Darren,' Colette called. Darren turned around, and McGregor signalled to the officer that he could allow him to linger in the corridor a moment.

'Finished your statement then?'

'For now. I've got to come back tomorrow. I need to sleep off that tranquiliser he gave me, honest to god my head is pounding. Feels like the worst hangover. And as for this leg.' He tried to raise the cast of his right leg, which made him wince with pain. 'Apparently it's not a bad break, but jogging is out for a while.'

The three of them looked at James Absalom. James Merchant.

'So, you went in there last night, knowing what he was going to do?'

'Not knowing. Reasonable suspicion. There was no other way to catch him.'

'Jesus. Is Absalom his middle name then? It's not on any of his ID.'

'Here's something else I learned from my theology course. Absalom was the favourite son of David, King of Israel and Judah. Characterised by his personal attractiveness, his lawless insolence, and his tragic fate.'

'Daddy issues.'

'Yep. He was desperate to please his father, fundamentally disagreed with his father, hated and revered his father, all in equal measure.'

Inside the interview room, James was deep in thought, but he looked, if anything, mildly elated.

'So, this is it then,' said Colette. 'Not even a society, just a family. They are sort of like modern survivalists, aren't they, living in their own parallel reality.'

'Don't you wish you were questioning him yourself then, Darren?' asked McGregor. 'Not making you homesick for this place?'

Darren shook his head, rocked on his crutches and looked down at his one remaining Nike shoe. 'I've spent more than enough time talking to that guy to last me a lifetime. He'll charm you, he'll bullshit you, he'll drive you round the bend. But he won't give you a straight answer. I don't think he's told the truth once in his life. Just remember this – he's far less intelligent than he sounds.'

'Really?'

'Really. Here's another razor for you. Hanlon's Razor. Never attribute to malice what can be explained by stupidity. How is he behaving in there?'

'He seems… interested. Like it's the next episode in his reality show. Most people would have killed themselves at that point. But he can't bear not to be around, to bask in the perverse glory of it. Knowing him, he'll be presenting his next TV show from prison.'

Lamb of God

And so it ends as it begins, on the eternal, eternally shifting sands of the beach. It had been a glorious June day, and the beach and dunes were still scattered with picnic-ers. They headed north, Darren and Helen, the docks behind them like giant sleeping robots, their lights just beginning to turn on for the evening. Ahead of them was nothing, just Liverpool's Iron Men looking out to a deep red sunset.

They wandered, not aimlessly, but capriciously, a walk designed for reflection upon strange events.

'I can't shake this feeling that something has been lost,' said Helen eventually. 'That's ridiculous, isn't it? Because you're safe, the mystery has been solved, they can't hurt anyone else. And a treasure trove of truths has been revealed. There're years of research ahead of multiple teams – police, archaeologists, historians, theologians like me... I mean, I should be relieved, excited, fascinated. Why do I feel a little sad?'

'I know what you mean. It's a myth shattered.'

'Not really. Because there was no myth, outside of their family – we didn't know about it.'

'I suppose conspiracy theories rarely get debunked. Because that's usually what they are – conspiracies. Maybe we like to think there are mysteries out there that will never be solved, strange things going on around us that we'll never know about. This one only survived that long because so few people were involved. There's usually a whistleblower at some point, but this was kept so close to home. And it was based on so little. That's the thing, it was so flimsy. It's mind-blowing. And if it wasn't so horrible, there's also something a little...I don't know, a little...'

'Poetic, maybe. There's something almost poetic about it, in the most macabre way of course. Keeping these hostages over the centuries. And they really thought it was the right thing to do. They weren't even motivated by malice, but by faith. They believed they themselves were the martyrs. And in fact, what a martyrdom, to deny themselves the possibility of Heaven, in order to allow others to go there. It's a sort of unlimited asceticism, the ultimate sacrifice. Let Heaven exist, even though we live in Hell.'

'I don't know. For James, the meaning had long been lost, I think. The ritual had become its own meaning. It was a piece of academic study for him, a piece of art. That's why he couldn't bear to keep it a secret.'

'I suppose I'm also a little jealous that I'm not one of the lucky people assigned to the case. Amber Rees is having a field day, she'll get a whole TV series out of those skeletons. And the archaeology department has set up shop over in Lunt, the ancient historians are on the manuscript, the history department have got hold of the library...'

'And it was only thanks to you that the society was discovered at all.'

'So I'm the martyr,' she laughed.

'Do you think there are other chapters of this society?' Darren asked. 'Elsewhere in the world? James says he'll never tell.'

'No. Because I think the Book Of Barabbas is a fake. I think they will discover it soon enough. From the excerpts they have published in the newspaper, I can already spot some anachronisms. For example, that business about living as a stranger on earth, that's a quote from Thomas A Kempis. Fifteenth century, not third century. I'm fairly sure it's a hoax.'

Their walk had taken them almost to Hall Road, and their clear pathway along the sand would soon be broken by the bricks of the Blitz Beach. They saw a boy running with his kite, a toddler watching from a pushchair, and a woman who waved to Darren.

'That's Elizabeth with her foster family,' he said.

'Oh yes. My goodness hasn't she grown? Darren. I know what I said, but how can the Book of Barabbas be a fake? Because it mentions Elizabeth. You saw what it said about virgin birth. Well, Chelsea McAllister was a virgin, artificially inseminated by Shepherd.'

'I think that's just… what do you call it? Synchronicity.'

'Maybe.'

They were quiet for a while, not wanting to explore this avenue of conversation further. There were indeed connections between this case and the Andrew Shepherd case, even if only the motives. All the perpetrators truly believed they were doing the right thing and, more than that, were sacrificing themselves. Denying themselves the possibility of Heaven. Darren wondered what it meant for him, now that he was beginning to feel an ominous complicity with Andrew Shepherd. If Darren felt, as he believed he did, a strange compulsion to protect this child, to stay close to her, what did that mean? Surely the logical conclusion, the ultimate implication, was that Andrew Shepherd had been right. That there really was a gene for sin, and Shepherd had succeeded in removing it from an unborn child. Did that make Shepherd a prophet? Or a god? Was he a redeemer of souls, or the opposite?

'It's a mindfuck,' he said out loud.

'It is indeed, as Mikko would say, a mindfuck,' agreed Helen, looking at him knowingly. 'So, what will the next chapter hold for you then, Darren?'

'I've still got another year of that degree, haven't I?'

'And then? You haven't exactly managed to stay away from police work.'

'I might work on being… less laconic. That's what Absalom called me.'

'I don't think you should change at all.'

'The thing is - the reason I saw through Absalom was my academic training. My bullshit detector was always strong, but Absalom took bullshit to a whole new level. And now I've learned how to better spot obscurantism. And I'm better read, so I was able to spot that almost everything he said was lifted from someone else.'

'Well, there you are. It will make you an even better policeman afterwards. Any regrets about leaving Thomas?'

He shook his head. 'Wasn't meant to be. Anyway, there are other reasons keeping me here.' He tried not to look at Elizabeth as he said this. Thomas had presented two alternative lives to him; the one in which he was the partner of a football hero, out in the open, beloved but with no privacy for the rest of his life, a life in which it would be impossible for him to be a detective. His privacy gone forever, his own city would become something else to him. The other, in which they lived in secret, and he would be so anonymous, in a foreign city, as to barely exist. Both options were nightmarish, but not for the obvious reasons. It was something to do with that child, Alfie, and the look in his eyes and what he somehow knew. And what he would do to Elizabeth. The only thing Darren knew for certain was that Alfie would reappear, somehow, in his life.

'But yeah, I'm ready for the next chapter. What about you?'

Helen put her hands to her belly that had not yet swollen. She looked out to the pale horizon.

'Yes. Ready for the next chapter.'

Chapter Thirty-Eight

The Book of Barabbas, or Liverpool Codex, partial text, c. 250 AD (disputed, currently under review at University of Liverpool), purple dyed vellum, multiple lacunae and insect-damage holes. Two fragmented pages.

And so, it came to pass that the notorious criminal Barabbas was cast into the wilderness by Pontius Pilate, to live out his days as a stranger on earth. He wandered into the desert and for many days and nights pondered the fortune of his escape, and wondered why Jesus had been crucified in his place.

But when he was weak with thirst and hunger, he cast off the scarlet thread from around his neck, and returned to his village, and to his wife and kin, resolving to live in quiet repentance and till the land.

One night a terrible storm befell his crops, and he looked in vain at his neighbours' fields around that were untouched by rain and wind.

He fell to his knees in the mud and the Lord spake unto him. Behold Barabbas, the goat for Azazel. Woe to you and to all men, Barabbas, for while my own son gave his blood to atone for the sins of all men, you could not do your part.

The bow of my wrath is bent, and the arrow made ready on the string, and justice bends the arrow at your heart, Barabbas.

It is nothing but my mere pleasure that keeps the arrow one moment from being made drunk with your blood.

There is nothing but my mere pleasure that keeps you and your deceitful heart out of Hell.

Should you not fear me? Should you not tremble in my presence?

I made the sand a boundary for the sea, an everlasting barrier it cannot cross

The waves may roll, but they cannot prevail, they may roar, but they cannot cross it.

And the Lord said 'Stand at the crossroads and look; ask for the ancient paths, ask where the good way is, and walk in it, and you will find rest for your souls. But you said I will not walk in it.'

Did you not see that you were Azazel, the second goat to be cast into the wilderness? Did you not see that you were to carry the sins of all men into the desert for all time?

Now this holy covenant has been broken, man must atone until the Son of Man returns.

As Adam and Eve's disobedience, your disobedience. As Eve's exquisite misery, your exquisite misery.

Your dim hope of rescue is the hope on which the universe shall rest. Someone must suffer for all eternity, on behalf of the human race.

Barabbas implored 'Father, what must I do to repent?'

'The Second Goat must perpetuate for all eternity. You were chosen in the image of my son. Every generation must choose a Second Goat, that must be in the image of my Son, at thirty-three years old. The Second Goat shall wear the scarlet thread.

Be thou a seeker of oblivion - go back into the wilderness and live a stranger on earth. This shall be your static voyage; the rest of your life shall be a long season in Hell. And tell your kin to find the next goat to be sacrificed after you. Who shall be identical in age to you and to Jesus.

You will be the void. Cover thyself in darkness and abide there forever. Wear a red thread to mark yourself as the Goat for Azazel.

To you will be ascribed all sins.

Cast thyself into the bottomless pit and set a seal upon it, that you shall deceive nations no more. If you fail, you shall end your life with a thorn to the heart as the thorns that pierced my Son.

This ritual shall persist until the three score generations should be fulfilled and the Son of Man will return by the second Virgin birth.

Thus, the balance in Heaven will be restored.'

This is the thing which the Lord hath commanded.

Chapter Thirty-Nine

Letter from Jeremiah Horrox to William Crabtree, 17th October 1639. Most of Horrox's papers were destroyed in the Civil War, some were taken by a brother to Ireland and never seen thereafter, and others were destroyed in the Great Fire of London 1666. The remainder passed into the hands of an antiquary, although almost all consisted of purely scientific observations and diagrams.

Carr House, Hoole
17th October 1639

My dear William,

How glad I am to hear that you are feeling better. I received your letter with much gratitude, and those musings on elliptical orbits warmed my heart in these cold autumn days.

I myself have been so hampered by my priestly duties that I have scarcely had time to enjoy the splendour of the celestial pageant. Although perhaps these two are not so very different; perhaps they are one and the same. The beautiful arrangement of the Heavenly bodies, which human science has demonstrated, must lead the mind to consider the wisdom which conceived and the power which executed such an epic. It is beyond unfortunate that religion and scientific study have been so posited against each other, because they are indeed one and the same, as you and I know. By the generosity of William Merchant, we will be able to do much more.

Lamb of God

Rapt in contemplation, I stand at my telescope for some time motionless, scarcely trusting my own senses, through an excess of joy. The telescope is almost another sense, another organ. Presenting to the human senses an abundance of new knowledge of which mankind has been ignorant since the dawn of time. Dreams and prophecies do thus much good, they make a man go on with boldness upon a danger or mistress. If he obtains, he attributes much to them; if he miscarries, he thinks no more of them.

I cannot conceal how much I am transported beyond myself with the Remembrance of those admiral Inventions which you shewed me. I should not have believed the world could have afforded such exquisite rarities and I know not how to stint my longing. Happier I had been, had I never known there were such Secrets, than to know no more, than that there are such. If I add only a hair breadth to the knowledge of others, I shall be contented.

My congregation here is composed primarily of, I suspect, recusants. I do have some sympathy, not only with their fear of persecution, but also with their grief. They crave the rituals that have been lost. Perhaps we all do. At the same time, they rather enjoy these Jeremiadic fire and brimstone sermons that my good uncle did make all the fashion.

Meanwhile our illustrious friend Williant Merchant craves treasure. Inspired by these Rosicrucians – and indeed who cannot be quite taken with the romance of it all – he fancies himself as the founder of some secret society with secret knowledge. He bids his sailors search every ship that comes in from the East for some ancient scroll that he can claim as his own.

And so, the stars align. A constellation of ideas is forming in my mind, rather like Venus and the Sun in my telescope, as to provide a fortuitous moment. I thought of using another of our parerga to solve both problems at once. We can give my congregation their ritual, their need for continual sacrifice, and Merchant his treasure book. Why not furnish them, and him, with that opportunity? Harness this recusancy of my dear parishioners, and let posterity be the witness of our result.

As Origen tells us, 'in the gospels events which did not take place at all are woven into the record of what literally did happen.' Then who is to say what did and did not happen, if it were all but parables? I had the fancy that we could set up our own apocryphal text, as a hypothesis. And perhaps arrive at some truth through the painstaking reconstruction of a text which may or may not be false. There is little to be lost, since if the devil does indeed exist, this will keep him at bay. For indeed what is a hypothesis, but a prophecy?

There has been much discussion recently in Cambridge and London about the establishment of a science of prophecy. Well, here is its first experiment. Richard Overton has been proposing a scientific experiment to test the immortality of the soul. Fox and Burroughs to test the miracle of the mass. These are far more absurd than a scheme that proposes to discover a hidden book of the Bible. There are rumours of the existence of the Book of Barabbas; indeed, it is probably already there, lying in some tomb beneath the desert. Or worse, has already ground to dust. So, what is the difference if we find it now rather than in a few centuries? Given the magnitudes of time to which we have been privy, centuries are mere drops in the ocean.

And indeed, it is a book that can solve the fundamental problem of the Reformation. Witches, malignant spirits and the Devil had been useful scapegoats for suffering. Who is to blame now? It is too cruel for humanity to blame ourselves. Let us ease their sense of guilt. This is the price paid for the gap between ideology and technology, and it is too high a price for the human spirit to pay. We can assist.

So perhaps between us we shall concoct a text – and apply to creativity and wit as we might usually apply to scientific study. And indeed, we can use scientific, should I even say alchemical, techniques to age this letter back to antiquity. I obtained a piece of parchment from a sailor fellow down at the seaport, which I believe I can easily manipulate. And I happen to have in my possession an old Aramaic dictionary that

Lamb of God

somehow travelled with me from Cambridge, so the translation shall not be too difficult. I shall then present it to the good Mr Merchant as a fortuitous treasure tumbled off one of his ships from the Holy Land.

Should human curiosity be allowed to play freely upon the works of creation? Yes, indeed, and it is our duty. Curiosity is the inheritance of mankind, bestowed upon us my God for our use in knowing Him. You will know better than most that there is no blasphemy intended in this experiment. It is beautiful to contemplate the manifold wisdom of my Creator in His wonderful operations. Heaven knows that the service to and glory of the Father Of All Lights is dearer to me than all the honours with which science could have crowned my youthful brow. The very hour when my calculations authorized me to expect the visible appearance of Venus upon the sun's disk was the hour of public worship. 150 years longer to wait if I missed it, and yet twice I suspended my operations and twice repaired to the house of God. The phenomenon was much to me, but the divine Author was infinitely more. Fortunately, after my second worshipful sojourn I was rewarded.

I believe we may set up this experiment with a clear conscience, since we will not be the ones to carry it out. We leave that to the interpretation of others. And so, this can be seen as an experiment in hermeneutics. It is our parerga, no, our duty, to create. Having been witness to immensity, to the wonder of the Heavens, it gives one a different sense of scale, don't you think? We are conducting astronomical experiments on a scale so great that it will be generations, centuries indeed, before the results are seen. And so, why should we not experiment with human thoughts in the same way? What if we conduct another experiment, that will last for generations?

Rather like the transit of Venus, the results will not be seen in the next lifetime or the lifetime after that. However, it has not stopped us from investigating, but only made us more considerate of posterity. We are but mere tools in a long experiment. A new concept of time, inspired by the stars; a religious experiment, to last through the ages. It seems to be that nothing could be more noble.

A literary experiment? A mind experiment? Or simply a trick between friends, conjured up by the exchange of letters. I thought you might join me in this endeavour. Jesus himself used satire, hyperbole, rhetoric, and so we can throw caution to the wind. Parody has no form – it assumes the shape it imitates. And so we are all parodies of ourselves. Parody can even transcend its original target and become something more powerful. The meaning depends on the reader's complicity, and so let Mr Merchant take responsibility for the meaning. Who knows what he will do with his mystical text?

We have become known, have we not, for proving seemingly absurd ideas? We have proved far more absurd ideas than this. Proved the existence of things that no-one can see. A new notion of knowledge. With science we can now know things we cannot see. Things that seem to fly in the face of reason. And so does God.

Do be careful to use the mail horses wisely. There is talk of war on the horizon, and indeed that in itself is rather fortuitous to our experiment, with prophecies which are already coming true. There have been prophecies about the apocalypse arriving in the 1650s, and our little project may take its place amongst them.

And so, my dear William, I bid you farewell until the next chapter in our journey.

Your friend,

Jeremiah Horrox

Thanks for reading *Lamb of God* by Catherine Fearns. Looking for your next read? Visit Northodox.co.uk for more genre-bending fiction.

Acknowlegements

Special thanks to Austrian Spencer for his invaluable advice and comments on the Lamb of God manuscript.

As always, thank you to the Reprobation readers whose continued support keeps me writing – the journey continues!

SUBMISSIONS ARE OPEN!

WRITER &
DEBUT AUTHOR   [ ]

NOVELS &
SHORT FICTION   [ ]

FROM OR LIVING
IN THE NORTH   [ ]

Printed in Great Britain
by Amazon

23425957R00148